Burke opened

All he saw was a to
oppressive it threat
Somewhere beyond
dark, a siren wailed
Disaster. Death.

No – something much, much worse.

The baby.

He groaned and curled into the stiff, creaky
mattress and pulled a pillow over his head,
tempted for a moment to press it against his
nose and mouth until he slipped into oblivion.

Waaa-uh-uh-waaa.

Damn Greenberg for throwing the tantrums
and pitching the ultimatums that had set him
on the road to this frozen wasteland. Damn
Fitz for handing him a map and waving
goodbye. Damn Nora for being here in the
first place.

And damn his sorry, aching, icicled self for
letting them all manoeuvre him into a mess
like this. Again.

Dear Reader,

I so enjoyed poking fun at Burke Elliot as I wrote the first book in the BRIGHT LIGHTS, BIG SKY series, *Millionaire Cowboy Seeks Wife,* that I was eager to indulge in a bit more fun at his expense in another book. Next time around, I promised myself, I wouldn't be satisfied with merely pricking that stiff and stuffy exterior. Next time I'd give him enough trouble to crack his considerable composure.

And it was clear who'd be the perfect woman to turn formal, orderly Burke's life upside down and inside out: Nora Daniels, the vivacious, emotional actress and soon-to-be divorcée and new mother. With her tempestuous manner and a life in a constant state of upheaval – what better woman to bring Burke to his knees?

But what made work on *Maybe, Baby* even more fun were the surprises lurking beneath those opposites-attract exteriors. It seems motherhood has steadied Nora, adding to her appeal. And it turned out Burke could be as passionate as Nora, in his own way.

I love to hear from my readers! Please come for a visit to my website at www.terrymclaughlin. com,or find me at www.wetnoodleposse.com or www.superauthors.com, or write to me at PO Box 5838, Eureka, CA 95502, USA.

Wishing you happily-ever-after reading,

Terry

Maybe, Baby

TERRY McLAUGHLIN

MILLS & BOON

Pure reading pleasure™

First published in Great Britain 2009
by Harlequin Mills & Boon Limited,
Eton House, 18-24 Paradise Road, Richmond, Surrey TW9 1SR

© Teresa A McLaughlin 2007

ISBN: 978 0 263 87369 6

38-0509

Harlequin Mills & Boon policy is to use papers that are
natural, renewable and recyclable products and made from
wood grown in sustainable forests. The logging and
manufacturing processes conform to the legal environmental
regulations of the country of origin.

Printed and bound in Spain
by Litografia Rosés S.A., Barcelona

For Ashley

CHAPTER ONE

BURKE ELLIOT GLANCED UP from the tidy stack of paperwork on his neatly arranged desk as Hollywood superstar Fitz Kelleran strolled into his Paramount Studios bungalow.

"Hi, honey," said Fitz. "I'm home." He shut the door on the remains of a gloomy February day and pitched a faded duffel at the reception area sofa before heading toward the tiny office bathroom, shedding bits of wardrobe in his wake.

"Not again." Burke bit back a resigned sigh as he rose from his desk chair and followed. He'd spent four years as Fitz's personal assistant before the actor had promoted him to associate producer for his new film-production company. Four years salvaging bits and bobs of order and sanity from the chaos his friend tended to churn up wherever he went. "This is getting to be a bad habit."

"What's the matter?" Fitz twisted the taps

in the narrow shower and adjusted the temperature of the spray. "Bad day? Your date cancel out on you tonight? Don't tell me you're not glad to see me."

Burke plucked a tuxedo tie dangling from the edge of the pedestal sink. "Why do you insist on showering here several evenings each week? Why don't you use the facilities in your dressing room?"

"Saves time." Fitz dropped his pants and shot Burke a grin as he stepped into the steaming stall. "I can clean up and check in with you at the same time."

Burke tossed the tie on the crumpled black trousers lying on the tile floor and settled for a seat on the toilet lid. There was always business to discuss, now that he was fine-tuning the preproduction budget for Fitz's pet project, a remake of the classic Western, *The Virginian*.

Just as the bright promise of Southern California sunshine had lured Burke from London's drizzle, Fitz had lured him from a junior executive position in an accounting firm with promises of Hollywood adventures. He'd come full circle, back to a world of columns and ledgers, but he didn't mind—he'd always enjoyed arranging figures in orderly rows. And the fact that those figures represented movie production details had a certain appeal of its own.

"I suppose I should be grateful you're learning to manage your time more efficiently."

"I have to, now that you're not doing it for me."

"I offered to find a replacement, didn't I?" Burke nudged aside a discarded sock.

"What?"

"A replacement."

"For you?" Fitz smiled over the top of the shower door and scrubbed shampoo into wet blond hair. "If you're going to quit again, can you wait until I'm dry?"

"Never mind." Attempting a conversation with someone whose head was currently stuck beneath a water spigot was a pointless exercise.

A knock sounded at the outer office door moments before a pretty young wardrobe assistant let herself into the reception area. "Hey, Burke."

"Good evening, Heather. I assume you're here to collect Mr. Kelleran's things." He gathered a pile of black-and-white formal wear and deposited it in her outstretched arms. "I believe this is all of it."

"'All of it.'" She smiled as she repeated his words. "I just love that English accent."

She stood in place near the bathroom door, methodically checking each article. Behind them, the sound of water splattering against the shower tile explained her obvious attempt to delay her departure. Most women would engage in similar ploys to catch a glimpse of one of *People*'s sexiest men alive wearing little more than those famous dimples.

Burke moved back to his desk and frowned at the contract lying in an open folder.

"Burke?" asked Heather.

"Hmm?" He glanced over his shoulder, distracted. "Is something missing?"

"No, nothing." She dropped the clothes beside Fitz's duffel and stepped closer. "I was just wondering…are you doing anything tomorrow night?"

Tomorrow night. Friday. Burke rearranged the fit of his glasses over his nose, reexamining his conclusions and readjusting his expectations. Not Fitz, then. And Heather…

She'd always seemed to be well organized and levelheaded. Very nearly serene—and Burke considered serenity an extremely desirable trait in any woman. He'd also found her physically attractive, in the general and abstract manner he regarded casual female acquaintances who weren't appallingly otherwise. Now he turned to take a closer look.

"Burke," Fitz called from the next room.

"Tomorrow night?" asked Burke.

The shower door clicked open. "Are you still there?" asked Fitz.

"Yes," said Heather. Her smile warmed, hinting at a number of possibilities for an extremely pleasant evening.

The phone on the desk trilled.

"Excuse me," said Burke as Fitz stalked into the room with a long white towel wrapped around his waist. He reached behind him and grabbed the phone. "Burke Elliot speaking."

"Tell Kelleran he's a dead man," shouted Myron Greenberg in Burke's ear. Greenberg, Fitz's agent and partner in his film-production company, was never serene. "Got that, Elliot? A dead man."

"You can tell him yourself," said Burke, pulling the phone a few inches from his head to prevent damage to his hearing. "He's standing right here, dripping on my carpet."

Fitz snatched his duffel from the sofa and headed back to the bathroom, shutting the door behind him.

Heather's smile widened.

"I'm not going to waste my breath," said Greenberg. "I'm through talking to that lying piece of—"

"Myron." Burke pulled off his glasses and polished them with the clean cloth he kept for that purpose in his top desk drawer. "Did you, by any chance, have another purpose in mind for this call?"

"Don't give me any of that snotty Brit attitude," said Greenberg before launching into one of his trademark obscenity-laden tantrums.

Burke resettled his glasses and angled his hip against the desk. He set the receiver down beside him, where he could monitor Greenberg's spewing from a more comfortable distance. "Tomorrow night?" he asked again.

"Yeah." Heather leaned toward him and teased a bright red nail along the edge of his shirt front. "You seem like a busy guy. The kind of guy who might appreciate a quiet, home-cooked meal."

"Elliot? Elliot!" screamed a faintly static Greenberg.

"Excuse me, Heather." Burke picked up the phone. "Yes?"

"I want Nora's signature on that contract, and I want it now. Right now. Got that?" Greenberg's voice quivered with more venom than usual. "You tell Fitz he'd better come through on this, or I'm out. I mean it this time."

Burke seized Heather's hand as it crept toward his collar and brought her fingertips to his lips. Her fingers were smooth and smelled agreeably of rose-scented soap. "You have every right to be angry, Myron," he said in his soothing, reasonable voice. "This delay has been intolerable."

Greenberg hesitated as though he hadn't expected agreement on the matter. "You're damn right it has."

"I'll see to it myself that Fitz understands the level of your frustration." He curled Heather's fingers in his and tipped up her palm to brush his mouth over her warm, delicate wrist.

"You do that." Myron huffed and puffed some more, and then there was a moment of ominous silence. "What do you mean, 'the level of my frustration'? Is that some kind of shrink b.s.? You trying to *handle* me, Elliot?"

"Is it working?"

Greenberg snorted a humorless laugh. "You couldn't handle a corpse on Valium."

"I wonder, Myron, why would a corpse need Valium?" Burke knew if he met the agent's bluster with calm logic, he'd soon tire of the one-sided row.

Fitz cracked open the bathroom door and peeked through the slit. "Is that Greenberg?"

Burke offered him the phone, and the door snapped shut.

"What was that?" asked Greenberg.

"And why would I want to handle a corpse?" asked Burke as Heather tugged her hand loose to trail her fingers along his jaw. "If it were a fresh corpse, at a murder scene, for instance, the police might become upset if I tampered with any evidence pertaining to the crime. And if it weren't a fresh corpse…if it were, perhaps, in temporary storage at a mortuary somewhere—"

Click.

"About tomorrow night…" Burke dropped the phone on his desk and slid his hands around Heather's narrow waist. "Let me check my—"

"You can't make it," said Fitz. He strode back into the room, dressed in ragged jeans and a specimen from his ever-increasing collection of T-shirts advertising Montana businesses and events. This one sported a logo for an establishment with the unfortunate name of the Beaverhead Bar & Grill.

The actor tossed pairs of thick socks and work boots on the floor in front of the sofa and plopped down on the cushions to tug them on. "You've got a prior engagement."

Burke spread his hands in what he hoped would appear like abject disappointment and shrugged an apology to Heather. She gave him a sizzling smile, collected the discarded wardrobe bits and sashayed out of the office.

She'd be back. She, or someone just like her. He seemed never to lack a selection of female company for the weekend. Or for most weeknights, to be precise.

And he always tried to be very, very precise.

"What engagement?" he asked Fitz when she'd gone.

"You didn't mind, did you?" His friend tipped his head toward the door.

"Not really." Burke shrugged again. "I must admit the invitation took me by surprise. I thought she was looking in your direction."

Fitz yanked one last time at the laces on his boot and straightened. "I'm a married man."

"Do you actually think that will stop the pretty young things of this world from tossing their lures your way?"

"They're wasting their bait. I climbed out of that pond a long time ago."

"You make it sound as though it's been years," said Burke. "You've only been married a few months."

"Yeah." Fitz grinned. "And now I'm going to be a father."

"I'm surprised you waited this long to remind me."

Burke couldn't hide his own smile at his friend's infectious delight. Fitz had surprised everyone who knew him with his sudden marriage to a woman he'd met at a location shoot the previous summer, a widow with a twelve-year-old daughter and a tangle of connections to a loosely extended family. An even greater surprise was his immediate foray into fatherhood.

Fatherhood. Burke suppressed a shudder. "You usually find a way to introduce the topic into any discussion within the first five minutes."

"I was distracted." Fitz frowned. "And you'd better not mention anything about that pond stuff to Ellie."

"I know better than to say anything at all about other women when your wife is within hearing range."

Tough, fiery Ellie Harrison Kelleran had no patience with Fitz's tendency to stumble into the tabloids. And because the man was head-over-boot-heels in love with her, he tried his best to maintain his balance and avoid any misunderstandings that might be construed as misadventures.

Ironically, the person of most interest to the press of late was Ellie, a petite redhead who'd caught the eye and captured the heart of Hollywood's most eligible bachelor. But the immense size and remote location of Granite Ridge Ranch, Fitz and Ellie's home in Southwest Montana, prevented the press from prying too deeply into their private lives.

"What engagement?" Burke asked again.

"Not an engagement, exactly. More like an assignment." Fitz stood and headed toward the miniscule kitchen. He selected one of the beers he himself had stocked in the cubelike refrigerator and waved a bottle of water at Burke.

Burke shook his head. He had a feeling he wasn't going to like what he was about to hear. "And just what is this assignment?"

Fitz popped the bottle cap and took a long, slow sip. "What did Greenberg want?"

"Your head on a platter."

"And?"

"Nora's signature on that contract."

The movie she'd filmed last summer in Montana with Fitz would open soon, and all indications were it was going to open big. She had her choice of scripts right now, and Fitz and Greenberg were pressuring her to choose theirs.

His, actually. Burke was the one who'd chosen the script for the classic screwball comedy, sold his bosses on the idea and secured the studio's blessing to launch the presale phase of production. He was the one who'd suggested Nora for the lead.

Nora Daniels was an actress poised on the brink of stardom. Men loved her lush, exotic features; women loved her sparkling, impetuous personality. Everyone loved her story: the daughter of an Argentinian heiress and an Irish entrepreneur who'd eloped to New York and gambled away their fortunes on a series of bad investments. When their marriage had crumbled, they'd both fled the country in the company of wealthier partners and left their beautiful baby daughter in the erratic care of a series of nannies and tutors, in a succession of hotels and flats.

At sixteen, she'd ditched an afternoon ballet lesson to sneak into a Broadway theater during an open call. Her audition performance had become a legend.

Audiences were enthralled with her style and flash, and she floated easily from the stage to the screen and back again. So far she'd preferred supporting roles, selecting those that would showcase her talent without compromising the progress of her career. She chose her work situations with equal care, seeking the company of an intimate group of friends, finding at rehearsals and on sets the relationships she'd craved during her childhood.

Two years ago the thirty-year-old actress had married an ambitious businessman, a restaurateur who'd assembled a talented staff in a stylish establishment, attracting a chic clientele. She'd believed she'd found a man who'd give her a family and a home. Instead, he'd deserted her when she was three months pregnant, leaving her alone in the house she'd purchased for them both.

Fitz's shoulders lifted and fell in a deep sigh. "She's talking about putting her house on the market."

Burke stilled. "Sorry?"

"Her house. The one in the Hills."

"She won't do it." Burke shoved off the desk and strode to the window, staring blindly at the glare of security lights on wet, black pavement. "She loves that house. It took her years to find it."

His lips twitched at the image of Nora dragging her samples about in the bulging handbags she preferred, driving them all insane with her constant requests for opinions about wallpapers and fabrics. "It's going to take her years to redecorate it."

"I don't think she's coming back."

"Back here?" Burke felt as though he'd been run through with a lance of ice. "But— but she lives here."

"She hasn't lived here since Thanksgiving." Fitz set his bottle on the counter with a loud clink. "She's dug in so deep in the guest cabin I don't think I could blast her loose with a stack of dynamite."

"You're the one who invited her." Burke turned and aimed an accusing look at his friend. "'Come for the holidays,' you said. 'Stay as long as you want.'"

"I didn't invite her," said Fitz. "That was Jenna's doing."

Nora had struck up a friendship with Fitz's

mother-in-law during the location shoot. Burke suspected Jenna Harrison Winterhawk had played a valuable supporting role for Nora during her pregnancy, and had probably continued in that role since Nora had given birth, in Montana, to a daughter of her own. Jenna was probably serving as a real-life model for the kind of mother Nora had never known.

"You were the one who told her she could stay," Burke pointed out.

"I didn't think she would!" Fitz flung his arms wide as he paced. "She's been there nearly four months. Four months!"

"I know how long it's been."

Burke slipped his hands into his pockets. He'd missed her, oddly enough. He'd never thought he'd admit such a thing to himself, but he did.

He'd missed her energetic conversation and her lusty laugh, the way she could sweep into a room like a whirlwind and set things spiraling out of control. He'd enjoyed the way she'd shower him with praise for bailing her out of her latest spot of trouble, the way she'd bat her eyelashes at him like the outrageous flirt she was and tell him he was her knight in shining armor.

She deserved a knight, whether that man wore armor or not. She was a dear and special friend, and he treasured her for that as much as for her company.

"I'm surrounded, out there at the ranch." Fitz collapsed on the sofa, legs sprawling. "I'm surrounded by gestating, lactating, menstruating women."

"God." Burke moved to the refrigerator and snatched a bottle of water to wash away the disagreeable sensation that had crept up the back of his throat.

"Did I tell you Jody got her period?"

Burke nearly choked. "Did you hear me ask?"

"All those hormones." Fitz sighed. "The aches and pains. The tears."

Burke tipped the bottle back and swallowed again, hard. "When do you go back?"

"Not soon enough." Fitz slumped against the cushions. "God, I miss them."

"I suppose one does get used to being surrounded," said Burke, just to be polite, though he didn't see how such a thing was possible.

"Yeah, well, you'll get your chance."

Burke froze. "I beg your pardon."

"That's the assignment I was talking about."

"Fitz." Burke lowered his bottle. "You

can't seriously be suggesting what I think you're suggesting."

"I'm not suggesting anything. I'm telling you." He stared at Burke, and he was as serious as Burke had ever seen him. "Someone has to get Nora's signature on that contract."

"You're her friend." Burke hated the note of desperation in his voice, and he willed it away. "You live there. You like it there. You'll go for a visit, you'll ask her to come back and sign the contract. She'll do it for you."

"I've already asked her, several times." Fitz sank even lower on the sofa. "The last time I brought up the subject, I must have pushed a little too hard or said something the wrong way, because she—" he rubbed a hand over his eyes, his mouth twisting in a pained grimace "—she cried."

"God." Burke pinched the bridge of his nose, knocking his glasses out of place. "Let me get this straight. You want me to fly out to Montana in the dead of winter."

"It's not the dead of winter." Fitz shrugged. "Not exactly."

"But there will be snow. And temperatures below freezing."

"It doesn't feel that cold when you're working in it."

"Which I won't be doing, since I don't know how to do ranch work."

The thought of ranch work—of disgusting things done to half-wild animals that out-weighed a man by several hundred pounds, of incomprehensible chores involving tools and machinery that could mangle a body in innumerable ways, all accomplished in con-ditions reeking of manure and worse—made him draw a deep, calming breath.

Which was immediately followed by a second wave of dread. "You want me to walk into that stew of female biological processes and press a new mother for a business decision?"

Fitz nodded. "That just about sums it up, yeah."

"Why me?"

"Because you're you." Fitz gave him a re-assuring grin. "The original ice man. Mr. Calm-Cool-and-Collected. And because Nora trusts you."

"About that trust factor…" Burke dumped the remainder of his water down the tiny bar sink. "If I convince her to do this, will I be acting in her best interests?"

Fitz narrowed his eyes. "I don't think I like the implications in that question."

Burke met his friend's glare with one of his own. "I didn't think you would, but I thought it needed to be asked."

"All right." Fitz nodded. "Here's another question loaded with uncomfortable implications. If you *don't* push her to do this, will you be acting in your own best interests?"

Burke dropped his empty bottle in the dustbin. "Is my job at stake?"

"No, your job is secure."

"Because of my association with you?"

Fitz's silence was filled with implications.

"I think Greenberg resents that fact even more than my snotty Brit attitude."

"You leave Greenberg to me."

"I bloody well won't." Burke shoved his hands into his pockets before he was tempted to ram them into something else. "I know I wouldn't have this job if I hadn't started as your assistant. But I've got it now, and I intend to do it as well as I can. As well as you expect me to. As well as Greenberg thinks it should be done."

"So," said Fitz with a grin, "you're going to Montana."

"It appears I am." Burke lifted a hand to settle his glasses over his nose. "God help me."

CHAPTER TWO

NORA LOWERED her knitting needles to her lap with a mournful sigh. "It's snowing again."

Jenna twitched back one of the lace curtain panels draped in the deep, three-windowed bay in the second parlor of the Harrison family home. The beam of a lamp on the tea table at her side captured the silver threaded through her honey-gold hair and highlighted the tiny lines at the corners of her blue eyes as she peered at the view beyond the glass pane. Rolling pastureland, buried beneath several inches of snow, stretched to the timbered foothills of the Tobacco Root Mountains.

"So it is," she said in her muted Texas twang.

"Burke isn't used to driving in snow."

"Doesn't it snow in England?" Jenna turned her attention back to her own needlework project, a cross-stitch keepsake for one of the babies due in early summer. Her former daughter-in-law, Ellie, was expecting a baby a few weeks before her daughter, Maggie Hammond.

"Burke's from London," said Nora, though she didn't know much more about his past than that. "I'm sure they don't let the snow pile up in the streets there. And it's getting late. And colder. And I don't think he knows how to put on chains."

Jenna knotted a strand of pink floss and snipped off the end. "You seem mighty anxious about Burke's arrival."

"That's because I have a good idea why he's coming." And that idea, with its dark and complicated twists and turns, was enough to make her throat close up and her palms sweat. Facing Burke meant facing her insecurities about her future.

She scrunched the beginnings of a tiny sweater to the end of one needle before stabbing them both into a ball of fuzzy pink yarn. "It's like he and Fitz are playing the good cop, bad cop routine. And Burke's the bad cop."

She knew she was overacting it, wringing the situation for every dramatic drop. And from the look Jenna sent her, it was obvious that Jenna knew it, too. But an actress had to stretch every once in a while to stay in shape. Besides, her friends here at Granite Ridge often seemed amused by her excesses.

"Well, you don't have anything to worry about." Jenna tidied her things and set them aside. "You're not a criminal."

"No," said Nora. "Just a fugitive."

A door slammed on the far side of the rambling, Victorian-era house. "Gran!" called Ellie's daughter, Jody, a few moments later. "I got an A on my math test."

"I'd better go catch her," said Jenna, "before she and her aunt Maggie decide that's reason enough to celebrate and spoil their dinners. Those two can empty the cookie jar when their after-school snacking gets out of hand."

Nora glanced out the window again, fretting over the fat white flakes falling from a darkening sky. Burke was supposed to arrive in time for the evening meal, but perhaps the snowfall would delay him. Or maybe he'd lose his way. He hadn't been here since Fitz and Ellie's wedding, and things looked different under all that white.

They looked clean. Clean and pure, and

lovelier than anything she'd ever seen. Everyone she'd met here—and everyone back in California—had warned her that winter in Montana could be harsh, but Nora loved it. She loved everything about this place and the people who lived in it.

No one here measured her worth by her looks or her talent or her box office draw, no one criticized her choices or questioned her decisions. No one here expected her to be anything but herself—and they'd given her the space and the freedom to begin to rediscover who that person was.

Maybe she'd abused Fitz's hospitality a bit too long while hiding from Hollywood's spotlight through the worst days of her divorce. And maybe she'd relied on Jenna a bit too much for help with her baby. But she'd needed that time and that help while she prepared to face the next phase of her life and take the next steps in her career.

She hadn't figured on having to face Burke.

Fitz's long-suffering assistant had always been one of her favorite people, a man she could tease with a safe and sisterly affection. A paragon who could patiently smooth every wrinkle and methodically clip every loose thread. The idea that all that patient efficiency would soon be aimed in her direction was a bit unnerving.

"My, don't you look domestic." Maggie sauntered into the parlor, an oversized sugar cookie in one hand and a tall glass of milk in the other. "Seeing you like that makes me feel as warm and fuzzy as that yarn."

Nora smiled as she tucked her knitting into the tapestry satchel Jenna had given her for Christmas. Warm and fuzzy were the last words she'd choose to describe her friend. Maggie might have had her mother's coloring, but there was nothing soft or countrified about the woman who stood before her in a short-and-sassy layered hairstyle, a silk-and-velvet kimono-style top and pencil-slim designer jeans.

"Is that for me?" Nora reached for the snack Maggie offered. "My, aren't you generous."

"Only because I helped myself to plenty before I came out here. And I've got this." Maggie pulled another cookie from a deep pocket and sank into the chair Jenna had vacated, crossing her model-length legs. "Mom's fussing over dinner. When is Burke going to show?"

"Any minute now." Nora sipped the milk

and stared past the curtains. "If nothing happened to him."

"You mean, like a blizzard or an avalanche or some other natural disaster? That's about what it would take to stop him."

"He might get lost."

"Bet he's got GPS on that phone of his. He's got practically everything else, including the private numbers for every Hollywood exec, European fashion model and Fortune 500 zillionaire." Maggie's mouth turned up in a crooked grin. "It wouldn't surprise me if he had a gizmo in some pocket that holds a copy of the Encyclopaedia Britannica and the launch codes for our intercontinental ballistic missiles."

Nora's smile stretched around a bite of cookie. "You make him sound like a comic-book character."

"If the colored tights fit…" Maggie leaned back and stacked her stylish heeled boots on a needlepoint stool. "Actually, I think they'd fit pretty well. And look damn good on him, too."

"On Burke?"

Maggie wiggled her eyebrows. "I've always been a sucker for stud muffins in college prof glasses. And he's got that whole

British Clark Kent thing going for him—
capable but clueless. Makes me wonder if
he's Superman in bed."

"Burke?"

"Yes, Burke." Maggie smoothed her hands
over her barely noticeable pregnancy bump.
"Don't tell me you've never noticed."

"I've never looked." Nora stuffed the rest
of the cookie in her mouth and brushed
crumbs from her hands. "He's just a friend."

"Is that so?"

Maggie gave Nora a sly smile, and Nora
remembered that Maggie's husband, Wayne
Hammond, had once been "just a friend"
from her school days, before she'd left for
Chicago vowing never to return. Maggie had
taken a second, longer look at the rancher
next door when she'd returned home last
summer, newly divorced and needing a fresh
start. She'd found it here, teaching at the
local high school and living the kind of life
she'd thought she'd wanted to escape.

Another fugitive from the big city who'd
found a refuge in this small-town world.

"Look who just woke up from her nap."
Jody carried Nora's three-month-old
daughter, Ashley, into the parlor. "I changed
her diaper already."

"Thanks, hon." Nora set her glass on the dainty mahogany tea table beside her. "I didn't hear her wake up."

"That's 'cause she was sucking her thumb again." Jody shifted the baby into Nora's arms and then straightened, shoving reddish bangs out of her dark hazel eyes. "She was just lying there, staring at me and sucking away. Slurp, slurp."

"Hello, sweetheart," Nora murmured. "Are you hungry?"

Ashley stared into her face as if the question were the most important thing she'd ever considered, and Nora's heart swelled against her ribs in an intensely painful and wonderful habit. Her daughter—her gorgeous, brilliant, marvelous daughter. She never tired of gazing at the frilly black ringlets springing out in every direction, at that turned-up button of a nose, at those wide, dark eyes. Her very own miracle.

"Here." Jody handed her a small quilt and two fresh cloth diapers. "I'll go get more."

"I think this will be enough for a while."

"The way that kid spits up?" Jody wrinkled her freckled nose in disgust. "I'll just bring in the load from the dryer. Might as well save yourself the trouble of folding them."

"Auntie Jody thinks you're an awful lot of trouble," Nora crooned as she unfastened the buttons of her blouse.

"I'm not the only one," said Jody. "Fitz calls her Upchuck Charlie."

"I hadn't heard that one." Maggie switched off the nursery monitor perched near Jenna's things on the tiny lamp table. "The night before he left, he was calling her Suzie Oozie."

"That's when her diaper leaked all over his shirt."

"The only thing I haven't heard him call her is *Ashley*," said Maggie.

Nora settled the baby against her breast and adjusted the quilt across her lap. Behind her, the tall case clock chimed the hour. She glanced toward the window again, searching for a car on the long ranch road.

Jody peered over Nora's shoulder to watch Ashley nurse. "She sure is a sweetie."

"Yes, she is."

"Pretty, too. She looks just like her mama."

Nora reached back and squeezed Jody's fingers where they rested on her shoulder. "Thanks for checking on her."

"No biggie. She snores, though."

"She does not."

"Yes, she does." Jody demonstrated with

some snuffles and snorts. "And she grunts like a pig when she starts to wake up. I could hardly concentrate on my homework."

The electronic tune of a cell phone—a more likely source for Jody's difficulty finishing her assignments—jangled in her pocket, and she checked the screen as she exited the room.

Nora tipped her head against the deeply tufted chair, her thoughts drifting with the snowflakes tumbling through the streaks of lantern light beyond the porch roof eaves. Outside, the ranch dogs barked and scrambled across the wraparound porch and bounded down to the wide gravel drive. A few moments later, pale headlights swept across the turn at the bottom of the knoll.

"Looks like he made it." Maggie stood and leaned a shoulder against the thick window trim. "Wonder how long he'll tough it out."

Jenna rushed into the parlor, wiping her hands on her apron. "That must be Burke. And Will just called with bad news about the water heater."

"What about it?" asked Maggie.

"Fitz asked me to open Will's old place for Burke," said Jenna. Will Winterhawk had married her last fall and moved from the foreman's cabin into the family home. "But Will says the water heater needs to be replaced. Pete's Hardware doesn't have the right model in stock, and now it's too late to drive to Sheridan to get one." She smoothed her apron. "I hope Burke doesn't mind staying in the guest room tonight."

"As long as he doesn't mind sharing a bathroom down the hall with four other people," said Maggie.

Nora shifted Ashley and lifted the quilt over her shoulder to loosely cover her. "If he doesn't like that idea, he can always drive back to town and find a place there."

She wasn't sure she liked the idea of Burke camped out at the house. Or on the ranch. Or in the state, for that matter.

But in the next moment, she felt guilty about the fact that most of the extended Harrison clan was crowded into this one house, while she and her baby shared one of the three rooms in Ellie's former home, the guest cabin a mile down the ranch road. There was plenty of space there for Burke, if he wanted it. She could keep an eye on him if she kept him close, and he could see for himself how happy she was here in Montana.

Ashley gurgled and whooped, and Nora

eased her embrace and ordered herself to relax.

"He's got a place right here," said Jenna. "It shouldn't be a problem. He's practically family."

"Hard to tell where he's going to want to stay," said Maggie, "except for somewhere else."

"He doesn't like it here, does he?" Jenna shook her head. "The poor man." She continued into the front parlor, heading toward the entry.

A dark gray SUV pulled into view, and the dogs danced around to the driver's-side door.

"Uh-oh, here comes Rowdy," said Maggie with a grin. "This is going to be interesting."

Nora tipped forward as far as she could and watched the driver's-side door of the rental car swing open. One long leg stretched toward the ground, and in the next moment Rowdy, the newest ranch mongrel adopted by one of the hands, rushed forward and sank his puppy teeth into the fabric of thin dress slacks. Burke tried shaking him off, but that made the game more fun.

Jenna stepped off the porch and made her way to the car. Nora couldn't hear what she was saying, but she guessed Jenna was trying to strike a ladylike balance between welcoming her guest and cussing at the dogs. Burke emerged from the car and stood, stiff and stoic, above the maelstrom of tails and paws and flying snow at his feet. He said something to Jenna with a formal nod and then stared at Rowdy, who'd released his toothy grip on Burke's pants only to replace it with a more intimate embrace of his leg.

"What a welcome," said Maggie with a laugh. "Poor Burke."

Nora dropped the quilt to switch Ashley to her other side, and then carefully covered them both again. She glanced up in time to see Burke stalk to the car's rear, yank open the hatchback and reach inside to collect a briefcase. Rowdy jumped up for one last nip at butt level, and Burke lost traction on the slick white snow coating the gravel and rammed his shin against the back fender.

She winced and shook her head. And then she remembered why he'd come, and she narrowed her eyes. Poor, poor Burke wasn't going to enjoy this visit at all.

A FEW MINUTES LATER, after Maggie had followed Jenna into the kitchen to help with the last of the dinner preparations, Nora heard the massive front door of the ranch house close with a *whump,* and then Burke appeared in the high, arched parlor doorway. Melting flakes dotted the creases of a blue parka he must have pulled from the rack in Butte. The white shirt collar poking through the neck opening was tugged awkwardly to one side, and one Rowdy-mangled pant leg was wet and twisted, riding crookedly up a dark gray sock. Caked with patches of white, his black dress shoes looked soaked through.

He'd obviously plowed a hand through his thick black hair more than once, making it stand out in uneven layers. One loose strand drooped over an eyebrow to brush against the edge of his glasses, and his nose was red from the cold. That amazingly perfect British complexion of his looked paler than usual, making the spots of color edging his angular cheekbones a vivid contrast. When he reached up to straighten his glasses over dark, deep-set eyes, he seemed very tired, and very disgruntled and, oh, so very dear.

He was a dear. He'd always been her friend and, until this moment, her protector. She wondered how he'd manage the shift in their relationship, how she'd deal with the same thing, and she shivered. He'd be a focused and tenacious adversary. She hoped their friendship would survive the coming days.

"Hello, Nora," he said in his low, slightly gruff voice.

"Hello, Burke." She lifted the quilt higher over her shoulder. "I hope your trip wasn't too bad."

"No. Not at all." His lips thinned with the hint of a grimace, and she remembered how much he hated to travel. "Everything went according to schedule," he said.

Ashley kicked at the quilt, and Burke stared for a moment at the tented spot before meeting Nora's gaze again. He cleared his throat.

"I hope you're hungry," she said. "Jenna's been cooking all afternoon."

"Whatever it is, it smells delicious."

"That's pecan pie, I think."

Ashley whooped and tugged at the cover.

He flicked another glance at the quilt. "Is that your baby under there?"

"Yes." Nora smiled. "I'll show her to you in a few minutes."

"Is there something—" Burke frowned and straightened. "Is she ill?"

"She's fine." Nora's smile widened. "She's nursing."

"Nursing?"

Nora could see the moment Burke understood what nursing meant. The red spots on his cheeks deepened and spread.

"I see," he said. "I mean, I don't. That is, I don't want to see, if that's all right. Not that I don't want to see the baby—I just don't want to see you. No—I mean, I do want to see you. Just not you and the baby. Together. Right now, that is."

"I know what you mean." Nora bit hard on her lip to kill a smile. "Don't worry. I don't want you to see right now, either."

"Well, then," he said with a stiff nod. "That's settled."

This was so strange, watching him deal with her in such a formal manner. And what was even stranger was the fact that the more ill at ease he appeared, the more relaxed she felt.

Things between them seemed reversed, somehow. Usually she was the one asking the questions, needing his help. Usually he was the one with the answers, the one in control.

"Why don't you take off that jacket and sit down?" She gestured at the empty chair across from her. "Dinner will be ready soon."

"While you—no, thank you."

Jody skidded into the room behind him. "Hey, Burke."

"Hello, Jody." His face eased into the first smile Nora had seen, deepening the grooves on either side of his mouth. "I've got a delivery for you. From Fitz."

"Shh." She glanced behind her, toward the entry. "You don't want Mom to find out. She'll skin us both."

Burke froze. "She will?"

Ellie had decided months ago that Fitz's habit of bringing presents back from his business trips to California needed to be broken. So far he'd been able to find a few ways to smuggle goods past her embargo, but it was always a dicey proposition.

"Is it in here?" Jody lifted his briefcase. "You can slip it to me while I help you carry your things to your room."

"My room?" He pushed his glasses up his nose. "I wasn't told I'd be staying here."

"Well, you are," said Jody as she headed toward the entry.

Burked turned to face Nora. "Fitz mentioned a small cabin."

"Will's old place. The water heater's broken."

"I've no hot water?"

"That's what Jenna said."

Ashley squawked and kicked at the quilt, and Nora struggled to button her blouse beneath the cover. "Will went into town today to get a replacement, but they didn't have what he needed. It won't be fixed until tomorrow."

"Then I'm to stay here, in this house?"

"You could go back to town, but the snow is coming down pretty fast now." She gave up on the buttons and lifted Ashley against her shoulder, still beneath the quilt, rubbing her back and hoping for a quick, neat burp. "Do you have chains?"

"For the tires, you mean?" He frowned. "There's a box in the back of the car."

"Do you know how to put them on?"

"I'm sure I can follow the directions." He closed his eyes, and his glasses slipped crookedly as he pinched at his nose. "Isn't there a snowplow service of some sort?"

"For the main roads. But it doesn't come out to Granite Ridge. And you might still need the chains."

Ashley burped. A loud, liquidy burp. The kind that meant lots of slightly curdled milk coming back up. A familiar warm, wet sensation slid over the edge of the cloth diaper and down the front of Nora's blouse.

"Isn't there another alternative?" asked Burke.

"Yes, there is." Nora folded the quilt down to reveal Ashley, her curly baby hair sticking up in places, her cheeks bright pink from the warmth beneath the cover. One side of her face was smeared with spit-up, as was the front of her yellow print sleeper. Her head wobbled a bit as she craned her neck to get a better look at Burke, and then she burped again—another long, wet, gurgly sound effect to accompany the stuff that spattered over Nora's lap and dripped to the floor.

"You could stay with the baby and me," said Nora.

CHAPTER THREE

BURKE TOOK HIS SEAT in the Harrison family's spacious dining room later that evening and surveyed the crowd gathered around the lake-sized table. Ellie and Will formed a cozy corner to his left, their voices low as they discussed scheduling changes involving an injured member of the ranch crew and the season's calving chores. Jody and Jenna sat to his right, negotiating the details of Jody's plans for a sleepover party. Across the table, Nora laughed at Maggie's description of a classroom incident while Wayne, Maggie's husband, paced behind them with Nora's squalling baby in his arms.

The table was set with thick, homey china and daffodils crowded in a fat pitcher, and the serving platters were heaped with delicious-looking food. The wine in Burke's goblet, which Wayne had contributed from his cellar, was a surprisingly good cabernet. At least

Burke could be assured of one thing: he wouldn't go hungry during his stay.

If only the din weren't enough to obliterate his appetite.

The baby ceased its howling for a moment, and a wide smile creased Wayne's rugged features as he lifted its face close to his and nuzzled its nose. "That's my girl," he said in his soft voice as he carried the kicking, writhing bundle toward the dimly lit parlor adjoining the dining room. "You were just waiting for your uncle Wayne to figure things out."

"Here, Burke," said Jody as she handed him a platter piled with thick slices of glazed ham. "And please pass the sweet potatoes down to Will when you get a chance."

He noticed the others were helping themselves to servings of beet salad, home-preserved peaches, dilled carrots, baked-bean casserole and corn bread. "Aren't we going to wait for Wayne to join us?"

"He's got Ashley."

"Yes, but—"

"He'll give someone else a turn in a minute," she said, handing him a pottery jar filled with some kind of aromatic relish. "He likes her. Besides, he says he needs the practice."

Burke didn't understand why anyone

would want to spend one minute more than necessary practicing to have his eardrums damaged.

"You'll get a turn, too," Jody said.

"Thank you, but that's not—"

"Excuse me, Burke." Nora fluttered impossibly thick lashes at him from across the table. "Could you please pass the butter?"

She looked lovely tonight, he thought, dazzled by her presence. He knew she was doing the dazzling bit on purpose, and he supposed he should be immune to it by now. But she was so bloody good at it.

She'd changed her top and pinned up her hair. A few wavy black tendrils wisped about her face and tumbled to drape along her long, shapely neck. Those impossibly dark almond-shaped eyes were somehow more exotic than ever without layers of makeup, and her famously pouty lips shimmered a clean, glossy pink. Motherhood had accentuated her mouthwatering curves, enough to send any man to his knees. She was a fresh-scrubbed Gypsy temptress, a siren in a white T-shirt and jeans, radiating so much charisma across the table he was afraid he'd burn to cinders in the heat.

"Burke?"

"Yes. Sorry." He snatched up the butter and handed it to Ellie to pass along.

Wayne lowered the baby into Maggie's arms and took his seat at the table.

"Have you heard from Fitz today?" Burke asked Ellie.

"Nope."

"He hasn't called you?"

"He knows better than to call me while I'm working." Ellie shrugged. "Just like I know better than to call him when he's on the set."

Burke was no stranger to Fitz's odd aversion to the phone—serving as a human message machine had been one of Burke's most important duties during his years as an assistant.

Maggie handed the baby to Jenna.

"He called me," Jody told Burke. "He wanted to know if you'd gotten here yet."

"Checking up on me, was he?"

"Uh, that's right." Jody gave him a look that reminded him he was a conspirator in the smuggling operation. "I told him you got here safe and sound."

The talk around the table turned to the day's local news. A fender bender on the town's main street, an injured basketball star denting the high-school team's chance at a division championship. A herd of elk damaging a fence line between Granite Ridge and the Hammonds' ranch.

The baby got passed to Jody, who stood and paced one slow, bobbing circuit around the table before returning to Burke's side.

"It's your turn," she said.

"My turn for what?"

"Diaper derby. Whoever's holding her when she poops has to change her diaper. Here."

"But I don't think—that is, I've never—"

I've never held a baby.

"Jody," said Jenna, "He doesn't—"

"Let him have a turn," said Nora. "He hasn't had a chance to hold her since he arrived. Have you, Burke?"

Her stare was a toxic mixture of guilt-inducing pleading and cool challenge. No hope of wiggling out of the situation. He shoved his chair back and prepared to deal with the inevitable.

"Put one hand here," said Jody, grabbing one of his hands and sliding it under the baby's head. "You don't want to let her head drop."

He was afraid to ask why.

"And here," she continued, guiding his other hand toward the baby's hips as she shifted the wiggling parcel into his arms, "support her back, like this."

His every instinct screamed at him to hand it back, now, before he suffered a massive stroke and dropped it or experienced a freak muscle spasm that caused him to pitch it across the room, but if he moved too quickly its head would hit the floor, or its spine might snap in two, and Nora would be destroyed by grief, and he'd never forgive himself. So he did the next-best thing and pulled it close to his body, the way he'd seen the others hold it.

A tiny foot pummeled his stomach, and tiny fingers stretched and closed around invisible items. And then its face puckered in a ghastly grimace, and it flushed a rapid, unnerving shade of purply red.

"Uh-oh," said Jody.

"What?" Burke was afraid to move, afraid to take his next breath. "What is it?"

"She's winding up for a big one."

"A big what?"

He glanced around the table, but no one else seemed to care what was happening. Apparently infant apoplexy was a common occurrence.

"You'll find out," said Jody, and she took her seat and resumed her meal.

The baby scrunched its features in an expression that would have put a facial contortionist to shame and flexed its back a bit. And then a most disturbing sound, a gelatinous, oozing kind of putt-putt emanated from the general area of the baby's bottom as something unpleasantly hot seemed to gush into his hand, though it was separated from the infant's skin by layers of nappy and clothing.

Burke had difficulty swallowing. "I think I just lost."

"Don't worry." Nora dabbed at her mouth and rose from her seat. "We wouldn't inflict a diaper change on a guest his first night here."

"My first night?" Burke regretted the weak and pleading tone of his voice, but the memory of what had just slid into a space a fraction of an inch from his palm was still fresh.

Literally.

"I don't suppose guest status could be extended indefinitely?" he asked.

"You don't have to do anything you don't want to." Jenna leveled a warning look at the others around the table. "You're not exactly family, although I certainly hope you'll come to feel as comfortable with us all as if you were."

He looked down at what he was holding and prayed that would never happen.

"Come here, sweetie." Nora scooped up the baby and settled it against her. "Mama will take care of you."

Its little face peeked over Nora's shoulder, taunting him.

Burke picked up his fork and regarded it with a frown. He seemed to have lost his appetite.

Bloody hell.

AFTER DINNER Nora had faced a quiet consultation with Will, who was worried about the worsening driving conditions, followed by a brief argument with Jenna, who didn't approve of the sleeping arrangements. Now she stood shivering in the amber band of light streaming from the back porch, having second thoughts about her stubborn defense of her impromptu invitation.

Ashley howled in protest as Burke lifted her carrier into the tight rear cab area of Nora's pickup truck and wedged it into the car seat base. He cracked the back of his head on the low door frame as he backed out.

"*Ouch,*" she said.

"That's my line, isn't it?" He rubbed his

head, frowning at the truck as Ashley continued to fuss. "Where did you get this?"

"I bought it from a cowpoke in Dillon who'd had a run of bad luck in a poker game."

Burke lowered his hand and stared at her.

"Okay," she said with a grin. "I made up the part about the poker."

"I'm sorry to hear that." He hunched his shoulders against a gust of snow-flecked wind. "It was the only part of the story that made any sense."

"It's a good little truck. Not much to look at, but dependable."

"I'll take your word for it," he muttered as he crunched across the snow toward his SUV.

Ashley's cries grew in volume during the winding drive along the narrow ranch road and the creek bridge, and by the time the cabin's lights winked into view through a stand of naked aspens, she'd worked herself into a tearful temper.

Burke pulled into a space beside the truck and waited while Nora unstrapped the carrier from the cab.

"Is she always like this?" Burke's expression was set in a stoic cast as he pulled a suitcase and garment bag from the back of his car.

"She's hungry."

"She just ate."

"Babies need to eat every few hours. Round the clock."

With Ashley complaining loudly, Nora gave Burke a quick tour of the compact cabin and handed him linens to make up a bed in one of the available rooms. She rearranged the clutter in the bathroom they'd share, clearing a spot for his things, and then she excused herself to see to the baby's needs.

She settled with a sigh into the big rocker she'd dragged into the cabin's largest bedroom and tried to lose herself in the peace of the moment, to be thankful for her daughter and to appreciate her good fortune as she always did during their quiet times together. But tonight her thoughts returned to the men in orbit around her, each exerting a gravitational force of his own. Ken, the ex-husband who'd been so entranced by his celebrity fiancée but disappointed with his working-actress wife. Fitz, the superstar friend with the supersized heart who'd offered her shelter.

And Burke, the tall, dark and brooding man unpacking his bags in the small room next door.

The long evening had exhausted Ashley, and she drifted to sleep as she nursed. Nora gently lowered her into the crib and bent to kiss her good-night. Then she slipped out of her clothes and pulled on a practical flannel gown and a splashy silk robe, bracing herself to deal with whatever Burke might decide to discuss this evening.

She found him standing in the middle of the open front room, staring at the laptop in his hands with a frown.

"Is something wrong?" she asked.

"Do you have a printer?"

"A printer?"

"For your computer."

"I don't have a computer."

"And I suppose that means you don't know whether or not you have an Internet connection."

"No," she said with a shrug. "Sorry."

He closed his eyes and squeezed at the bridge of his nose, knocking his glasses askew. "I can probably rig something up with my cell phone."

"I don't think that'll work here."

"Why not?"

"My cell works fine at the main ranch house. But this cabin seems to be tucked into some little pocket that doesn't get any reception. Don't worry, I have a regular phone," she added quickly.

"But no cell reception."

"That's not a problem, is it?"

"No. No problem," he said, although the way his jaw clenched around the words told her he was lying through his gritted teeth.

"All settled in, then?" She opened the woodstove and lit the kindling. "Do you have everything else you need?"

"Yes, thank you."

"Would you like something to drink?"

"No, thank you."

"Help yourself to whatever's in the fridge."

"I will. Thank you."

"You're welcome." She glanced over her shoulder, waiting for him to say more—perhaps to thank her for a fourth time—but he stood very still, staring at the fire.

She pulled a log from the crate beside the stove and shoved it on top of the blazing kindling. "This will help keep the place warm tonight."

"Isn't there a furnace?"

"Yes. But this is nicer, don't you think?"

His silence told her precisely what he thought.

She turned to face him, twisting the ring on her right hand and willing herself not to scream away her tension. "Burke."

"Yes?"

"Are you waiting until tomorrow to start in on me?"

He shifted his impassive stare in her direction. "I'm not planning to start in on you."

"Oh, I see." She paced to the kitchen area and back. "You just decided on a whim to come out to Granite Ridge to work for a while. A change of scene, a different Internet connection. Is that right?"

"If you don't mind, I'd like to spend the evening chatting. As we used to." He set his computer on the small dining table tucked beneath a wide window and rested his hand on the dull metallic surface. "I've missed you."

She paused, studying him, waiting to see if his serious words and somber mood were some kind of clever trap. And in the next instant, she felt ashamed for looking for an ulterior motive. They were friends, after all. And she'd missed him, too.

"Tell me about Fitz." She folded her legs beneath her as she settled on one end of the sofa. "Has he been staying out of trouble?"

Burke lowered himself to the cushion beside her and leaned back with a sigh. "Fitz is playing the role of devoted husband and expectant father with such enthusiasm that it's beginning to grate on my nerves. I wish he'd try a more subtle approach to this rash of exemplary behavior."

She smiled and scooped her hair back. "Like you?"

Burke raised one eyebrow in his supercilious look. "I wasn't aware that my exemplary behavior was either overstated or abnormal."

"*No.*" Good old Burke, he could always make her laugh. She ran her hand down his arm in a teasing stroke. "I meant subtle. Like you."

Burke frowned. "Subtle is a difficult role for any actor."

She leaned toward him. "Even for me?"

"Especially for you."

"Are you saying I couldn't play it?"

"Only if it were a role." His face softened with a weary smile. "And then you'd be brilliant at it, as you always are."

She closed the small gap between them and smacked a loud kiss on the tip of his nose. "I love it when you lay it on thick."

"I'm only telling it like it is."

She laughed at the sound of that phrase uttered in his thickest, upper-crustiest accent. "And how's Greenberg?"

"Greenberg is his unsubtle and unexemplary self." Burke shook his head with a sigh. "His latest lover moved on to a soap actor, which hasn't improved his mood of late."

Nora tensed. She'd hoped the conversation wouldn't shift so soon to Hollywood business. But it was difficult for the two of them to avoid the topic for long.

"The preproduction budget for *The Virginian* is coming along as well as can be expected," he said, "considering all the difficulties inherent in a project of this scope." He frowned and shifted forward, his long fingers dangling between his knees. "Which means it's been a struggle getting Fitz to focus and getting Greenberg to relax."

"It's rough being caught in the middle."

"Yes, I suppose that's it."

The fire behind the stove grate snapped and roared. Burke twisted his fingers together and stared at the floor.

"Your daughter is very pretty," he said after a while.

"Thank you." Nora sighed and leaned her shoulder against the sofa back. She'd been waiting for him to mention her beautiful, precious daughter, waiting for him to lavish the praise she deserved. To lay it on thick.

But he hadn't even called her by her name yet. "Her name is Ashley."

"Yes. Ashley."

Nora smiled. Her name sounded heavenly when he spoke it in those plummy tones. "She'll be four months old in a couple of weeks."

"So soon."

"Yes, so soon. She's growing so fast, changing every day. Time seems to pass more quickly now."

"Yes, it does," he said. "Everything changes and moves on quickly, whether we want it to or not."

She tensed and twined her fingers through the sash of her robe, waiting for the first skirmish in the coming battle.

"Have you considered where you're going to go after you leave here?" he asked.

"I'm not leaving for a while yet."

"But you must have some idea."

"Of course I have ideas. Lots of them." She untangled her fingers and smoothed the ends of the sash across her lap. "Just nothing definite. Not yet, anyway."

He glanced at her with a frown. "Fitz told me you're thinking of putting your house up for sale."

"That's one of those ideas."

"But you love that house."

"Ken loved it, too."

"Ah." Burke took her hand and gave it a gentle squeeze. "I'm sorry for the unhappy memories."

"You don't have to be, since the ones you added were some of the best." She pulled her hand from his and gave it a friendly pat. "I had some good times there. And, yes, I loved it. I loved living there and trying my best to make it a home, because it was the first place I could call my own. But there'll be other places, and it's a great time to cash in on the investment. I could use the money from the sale."

"There are other ways to raise funds. Ways that would let you keep your house."

"Why are you so concerned about my house?"

"Because you were, at one time." He shifted on the sofa to face her. "Because I think you still are."

She stood and moved across the room to shove another piece of wood into the stove.

He was right, of course. But while she'd won the house in the divorce settlement, Ken had walked away with most of the cash needed for its upkeep. The thought of losing that house—the wisteria-covered porches, the sloping tiled roof, the tall windows and curved stairway, the dramatic sweeps and the intimate niches—twisted her heart like a rag and squeezed it dry.

Mentioning Ken like that, using the pain of her divorce like a shield had been a convenient way to deflect the issue and obscure the truth. It was easier to stay here, in Montana, than to deal with the fallout of her failed marriage in Hollywood. It was more tempting to consider moving on than to face going back. "Like I said, there are plenty of other houses out there. I don't mind looking. It's fun to wander through a place and try it on for size, to see if it fits. To imagine the possibilities."

"Where are you going to look next?"

"Why do you want to know?" She turned to face him. "Why do you have to know, tonight?"

His steady, searching stare sent a shiver up her spine, and she wrapped her arms around her waist.

"Sorry, Burke. I know I'm grouchy. I get

tired easily these days. Caring for Ashley takes a lot out of me. Literally," she added with a smile.

At her mention of her daughter, something awkward flickered across his features. He stood and brushed his hands over his slacks. "And I've kept you up too late. I'm sorry. It won't happen again."

"You don't have to apologize. You don't have to keep thanking me, and you don't have to be so damn—"

Her voice rose on a hot spike of temper, but she didn't care. Yes, she was tired, but mostly she was hurt, wounded by his reaction to Ashley; his lack of reaction, to be precise. Angry that he'd used her own house as the first salvo against her, and that he'd hit one of her most sensitive spots dead center with that first strike.

And worried that she didn't have an answer to his question about where she intended to live. How shortsighted and irresponsible she must seem. How pitiful.

"You don't have to watch your every step around me," she said at last.

"Is that what you think I'm doing?"

"Aren't you?"

"I wasn't aware of it."

"And you're so completely aware of everything, aren't you?"

He narrowed his eyes at her. "Including unsubtle behavior."

"I already told you—I'm tired and grouchy." She stormed into the kitchen area, her robe billowing about her legs, and snatched up the teakettle. She slapped at the faucet and ran water into the spout. "If you don't like my unsubtle behavior, you're welcome to stay elsewhere."

"Are you rescinding your invitation?"

"Don't worry." She slammed the kettle on a burner grate and whirled to face him. "I won't toss you out in the cold tonight."

"Neither of us has to worry, then. I'm sure that with a little practice, I can be as unthoughtful and ungrateful as you require."

He reached up and readjusted his glasses in one of those cool and controlled moves of his that normally made her itch to poke at his composure and tease him senseless. Tonight his attitude set her teeth on edge.

"However," he added, "if you change your mind, it appears it will still be quite cold enough for tossing me out tomorrow."

CHAPTER FOUR

WILL WINTERHAWK stretched with a sigh along one side of the four-poster bed in the room he shared with Jenna. He'd always looked forward to this time of day, when he could let his body and mind unwind, when he could switch off his focus on the ranch work and set his imagination loose to ease him into sleep and pleasant dreams.

For twenty years he'd passed most of his evenings with his nose buried in one of the books he treasured, keeping company with interesting characters and picking up some new ways of thinking about things. Now he spent his evenings with his wife, the woman he'd loved in secret through all those years.

He didn't miss the books so much, though he still managed to read more than most men he knew. Jenna was turning out to be one of the most interesting characters he'd ever known, and trying to figure out her ways of thinking about things was going to keep him occupied for longer than he could imagine.

And he deeply treasured the way they could ease each other into sleep and pleasant dreams.

But tonight Jenna's brisk motions as she scrubbed and creamed her way through her bedtime routine told him she needed a bit more time to unwind.

"I s'pose," he said, "I should drive over to the guest cabin in the morning and check up on those two. Make sure they've got enough wood for the stove and plenty of propane in the tank."

"He doesn't need to stay there after tonight."

She took a seat at the heirloom vanity and picked up her silver-handled brush. One thin strap of her silky blue gown slipped like a tease over her shoulder and made his mouth water.

"You'll have the water heater replaced by tomorrow afternoon," she said, shooting him a stern glance from the mirror.

"Maybe Burke will decide to stay right where he is."

"I don't think that's a good idea."

"You made that plenty clear earlier this evening." Watching the way that brush was getting tugged through her pretty gold-and-silver hair, Will figured she was still upset that her wishes in the matter had been dismissed. Jenna may have spent a lifetime cultivating a pleasant and easygoing facade, but underneath her soft, Southern debutante manner was a stubborn streak with a steel spine to support it.

And a big and generous heart, a heart that gathered folks deep inside and loved them hard and long, a heart that was prone to splinter a mite too easily when those she'd grown fond of drifted beyond her reach. To Jenna, home and family tended to blur together until they were one and the same, and she expended a great deal of energy to keep the whole of it corralled within the same geographical boundaries.

She'd made a habit of taking in strays, and she was well on the way to embracing Nora in much the same way she'd adopted Ellie when she was a girl—a casual acceptance, a growing bond, a maternal commitment. And now the comfort of that close relationship was threatened by a man from the outside who just might remove Nora from Jenna's tight family circle.

"I didn't mean to offend anyone." Jenna frowned at her reflection. "I just don't…well, you know what I think."

"Yes, I do." He traced the edge of an appliquéd leaf on the old quilt and waited for her to get around to confessing to the reasons behind her resentment of Burke's decision to bunk with Nora.

"You don't like the fact that he's staying with her, either." She shot him a dark look in the mirror. "And now you're going to lie awake half the night, worrying about the weather and whether he'll drive off the edge of the creek bridge tomorrow morning."

"Thank you, darlin', for being so solicitous about my worries." He smiled at both their reflections, noting again the vivid contrast his dark skin and black hair made against her fair features. "But I suspect you've got some of your own worries about the matter, too."

"His coming here is upsetting Nora."

"She didn't appear all that upset with the situation at dinner tonight."

"She was being polite. Making the best of the situation. She is an actress, you know."

"And a damn good one, from what I've seen." He smoothed a wide, tanned hand over the pastel spread. "She really got into the role, what with inviting him to stay at her place and all."

"Humph." Jenna dismissed that topic and warmed up another one. "And did you notice what was going on across the table tonight?"

He met her gaze. "I'm not sure you and I noticed the same things."

"Flirting." Her lips pressed together in a thin line of disapproval. "The two of them."

"Maybe I noticed some of that on Nora's part. Truth is, I don't pay it much mind anymore, seeing as how she simpers and flutters now and again just to keep her feminine wiles from going rusty." He frowned. "I can't say I know Burke well enough to judge his reactions. But I'd be hard-pressed to apply that label to any of his behavior tonight."

Jenna punished her hair with another series of short-tempered strokes. "I don't like the way he looks at her."

Will met her gaze in the mirror. "How does he look at her?"

"You know what I mean."

"Yes, I think I do." He sat up and shifted to the edge of the mattress. Last summer, before Jenna had agreed to marry him, they'd had a talk about the kinds of looks men and women gave each other. And then he'd kissed her and asked her to take a good, long look at him.

"All I saw tonight," he said, "was two old

friends getting together for the first time in several months."

Jenna tapped the brush against her hand. "That wasn't a completely friendly look I saw him giving her."

Will shrugged. "Maybe he's not feeling all that friendly about getting sent clear out here to fetch her back."

"That's not what I meant." Jenna set the brush down and turned to face him. "And she's not going back."

"Seems to me that's up to her to decide."

"If it's up to her to decide, then he wasted his time coming out here."

Will stared at his wife's mulish expression and hoped he wouldn't end up adding another trouble to his list of things to worry over tonight. "She'll have to leave eventually, you know."

"She doesn't want to."

"Has she discussed that with you?"

"Not in so many words."

"Jenna." Will stood and reached for her hand. "She can't stay here forever."

He waited patiently, and after a few seconds she surrendered to his silent request and turned to enclose her slim, pale fingers in his big, rough hand.

"She likes it here." Jenna's voice grew soft and wavery. "And she's been happy here."

"I'm glad to hear it. Means she'll come back for visits now and again."

Jenna stroked her thumb over a scar on his knuckle. "I don't want her to go, Will."

"I know you don't, darlin'."

"She'll take that sweet baby girl with her, and I won't get to see her grow up."

"You'll have a couple more babies to love in a few months."

"They won't be Ashley."

"No, they won't." He pulled her from her chair to wrap his arms around her waist and hug her close, and her gown quivered and shimmered and hinted at the womanly curves beneath the silk. "They'll probably sleep for more than an hour at a time and keep the milk they drink in their bellies, where it belongs. No fun at all."

She leaned her head against his shoulder, and he breathed in the scents of her shampoo and soap and creams. They brought to mind a meadow lush with wildflowers, a woman warmed in the summer sun.

"It won't be the same around here without her."

"No, I don't suppose it will," he said.

"It'll be a whole lot quieter and cleaner, that's for sure."

He guided her down, down to their soft bed, and he shifted over her to press a gentle kiss to the spot behind one ear, right where he'd watched her dab on some of that perfume he'd told her he liked so well.

Her pulse stuttered beneath his lips. "You'll miss her, too."

"I s'pose I will."

He skimmed his fingers across her shoulder, pushing the silk aside. "I have an idea or two about how we can keep those worries of ours off our minds for a while."

She lifted her arms to circle his neck. "You do, do you?"

"Yes, ma'am. I'm surprised you can't tell just by looking at me how friendly I'm feeling right now."

"Are you flirting with me, Will Winterhawk?"

He took one of her hands and pressed it to his bare chest. "I'm fluttering for you, Jenna. Just for you. Seems I always am."

BURKE OPENED HIS EYES to a tomblike blackness so oppressive it threatened to suffocate him. Somewhere beyond the boundaries of the dark a siren wailed its dirge. Suffering. Disaster. Death.

No. Something much, much worse.

The baby.

He groaned and curled into the stiff, creaky mattress and pulled a pillow over his head, tempted for a moment to press it against his nose and mouth until he slipped into oblivion.

Waaa-uh-uh-waaa.

Damn Greenberg for throwing the tantrums and pitching the ultimatums that had set him on the road to this frozen wasteland. Damn Fitz for handing him a map and waving goodbye. Damn Nora for being here in the first place.

And damn his sorry, aching, icicled self for letting them all maneuver him into a mess like this. Again.

He was a perfectly good associate pro— No, he was a bloody terrific associate producer. So terrific he'd already turned down a few offers to trade up. Greenberg's little empire would go down in flames without Burke there to douse the stray sparks, and Fitz would be quite put out.

Yes, quite. The actor was far more capable than he let on, but he'd invested years in cultivating his image of carefree, casual success. He wouldn't appreciate being caught out doing something as prosaic as paperwork.

Burke Elliot, enabler. Even the amateurs had roles to play in Hollywood, and he played his as well as any actor in the city. But he preferred to play it at his desk, in his tidy bungalow, with outlets for his office equipment and a phone with more than one line.

With a functional thermostat and a private bath.

He shoved a foot against the iron rail at the end of the too-short mattress and realized he couldn't feel his toes.

Frostbite, most likely. How tidy of nature to provide a natural anesthetic in case some backwoods carnivore decided to nibble on one's extremities.

Waaa. Waaa-uh-waaa.

"God." He rolled to his back and tugged a sloppy tangle of quilts around his chin, staring blindly at a wood plank ceiling he knew was festooned with solidified drips of resinous matter and ghostly tatters of cobwebs. The country style had so much natural charm to offer, if one knew where to look.

The baby wailed again, from the direction of the open room that served as entry, parlor, dining area and kitchen. One more minute, and he'd go out there, to see if Nora needed any help.

And what kind of assistance would he offer her? Feed the baby? Change its nappy? Ship it to a boarding school?

He sighed and rubbed a hand over his face, grimacing at the freeze-dried nubbin that was his nose. *Ashley.* The baby's name was Ashley. He didn't wish to be on more familiar terms with the child than necessary, but Nora seemed to require his active admiration and involvement.

Part of any producer's job, after all: making nice with the talent. And he valued his friendship with the actress enough to make more of an effort.

There. Silence.

Perhaps they'd both frozen to death.

He borrowed a few of Greenberg's nastiest swearwords as he tossed off the covers and reached for his glasses, and then swung his bare feet to the scratchy wool rug covering a portion of the wood floor. Tugging a sweater over his head, he made his way down the short hall to the front room, where a tropical wave of stove-heated air washed away his goose bumps.

Nora, swathed in her high-necked gown and a shawl-like wrap, rocked in the tall chair beside the stove and crooned an off-key tune in a slightly hoarse voice. She made a gorgeous Madonna, a Renaissance vision of ripe curves beneath the flowing folds of the soft fabric, of perfect features against pale skin. Her dreamy, ethereal expression as she stared at the child in her arms was as peaceful, as compelling as a timeless work of art. Her black hair tumbled and waved about her shoulders, thick and lustrous and practically begging a man to bury his fingers in its silky strands.

He scrubbed a hand over his face. Where had that last terrifying thought come from? He knew he wasn't sleepwalking through a nightmare—he was all too aware of the needlelike tingling in his toes as the blood began to circulate through them.

"Burke." She whispered his name with a finger against her lips. "I just got her to sleep."

"Congratulations."

He stood in the center of the room, uncertain of his next move. She sighed and leaned her head against the chair, and he noticed the dark smudges beneath her eyes.

"Can I get you anything?" he asked.

She smiled and shook her head. "No, thank you. I'm just going to sit here a while longer and enjoy the quiet." She shifted the baby slightly. "I'm sorry we woke you."

"You don't have to apologize."

"I don't?" One of her feathery brows arched up in amusement. "Don't you start getting sarcastic with me, buster. I'm the mom here. I'll send you to your room."

"You're not my mother."

"Doesn't matter."

"You're a good one. A good mother."

The rocker stilled. "Do you really think so?"

Yes, he did, but why had he blurted it out like that? Another renegade thought coming at him from an unknown source. He obviously wasn't himself tonight, speaking without thinking things through. "You're much more patient than I thought you'd be."

"Patient?"

"With the—" he waved his hand in a circle "—with the spitting up. And the crying. And—and everything."

"Oh." She frowned. "Thank you."

"I meant it as a compliment."

"I'm sure you did," she said, although she didn't seem all that convinced of the fact.

"Is it normal for a baby to be…to be so—"

"Annoying?"

"I'm sure she's not doing it on purpose."

Nora stared at him for a long moment. "Come here," she said at last. "You haven't had a chance to get a good look at her."

He was tempted to disagree, but he tiptoed across the room and moved to Nora's side to peer at the infant in her arms.

Asleep, Ashley was a different baby entirely. Pink and delicate, and…*amazing,* now that he had this chance to study her without any anxiety about holding her correctly or bracing for something unpleasant. Every feature that should be present was correctly in place—and each of them was an incredible, perfect miniature. He had never seen human hair so fine, curving in such interesting waves, or such a little nose turning up in such a wonderfully sculpted shape. The tiny spikes of her eyelashes spread in a soft crescent along cheeks that already showed the promise of her mother's lush curves, and her pink lips bowed with the hint of a killer pout. As he watched, her mouth moved in a silent rhythm.

"What is she doing?" he whispered. "Is she dreaming?"

"Maybe." Nora wrapped a fuzzy yellow

blanket more securely over the baby's shoulder. "I wonder what she dreams about. What she thinks."

"Why does she cry so much?" He shifted from behind Nora's chair so he could stare from a different angle. "Is she in pain?"

"A lot of the time, poor thing. She's colicky, always has been. She'll grow out of it eventually."

"Poor Ashley."

Nora looked up with a smile and reached for his hand, and he took hers and gave it a gentle squeeze.

Neither of them let go for a moment, and in the next moment it was too late—he was too aware of the feel of her hand in his to release it and return to the old ease between them. Her awkward tug as she pulled away told him she'd felt the same.

He rubbed one foot over the other, wondering how to make her smile again, how to undo this puzzling tension between them. He told himself they'd get things sorted out in the morning, when they'd both had a bit more sleep, but he couldn't think of an appropriate exit line.

"You can go back to bed now," she said. "We won't be making any more noise for a while, and you should grab some sleep while you have the chance."

"Is that what you do now? Grab sleep in snatches?"

"Yes."

"For how long?"

She stared at her sleeping child with an achingly tender smile and set the chair in motion again. "For as long as it takes."

He'd seen the smile he'd waited for, and now he was strangely sorry it was time to go. The expression on her face seemed to pierce right through him, reaching deep into a spot he hadn't known existed until it twinged with a bittersweet pain.

"Good night, then," he said.

"Good night, Burke."

Her low, throaty tune followed him down the cold, dim hallway.

CHAPTER FIVE

NORA SHOVED a hunk of hair behind one ear and frowned at the jumble of dishes in the sink and the meager pile of breakfast ingredients on the kitchen counter. She hadn't kept up with the housework, she'd forgotten she was running low on her emergency supply of breakfast basics, and now she had to share all her shortcomings with an unexpected guest.

A guest who wandered through her house in the middle of the night, intruding on her private time, the dark and quiet hours when she was most lonely, most vulnerable. She didn't want anyone to see her like that, with her pillow-mussed hair and her fatigue-tinged eyes, with her spit-up-stained nightgown and her ratty robe. And yet it had been good to know there was someone else there, someone who cared about her enough to come looking for her, to offer her assistance and reassurance.

She'd forgotten how supportive Burke could be. Had always been.

But before last night, they'd always spent their time together in small doses, in afternoons at Fitz's house or quick conversations at parties, in snatches of between-scene activity on the set or in a shared meal. In passing, really.

It wasn't until she'd been confronted by his things in her bathroom this morning—neatly arranged and organized—that she'd begun to consider the consequences of her impulsive invitation, to worry over the damage sharing such close quarters might do to their friendship. They were already dealing with a difficult situation. Why had she added another layer of stress to it?

And why had he agreed to the arrangement?

"Good morning."

She turned to see him standing in the hall doorway, looking adorably tense, his shower-damp hair slicked back and his briefcase dangling from one hand. The boots on his feet looked new enough to give him blisters, and his crisp white shirt was neatly tucked into jeans that looked so stiff they could probably stand on their own creased legs.

"Good morning," she said. "I hope you're not too hungry."

He frowned and pushed his glasses up his nose. "Why?"

"Because the snow might be too deep to get to the ranch house, and I don't have much to eat here."

He strode to the window above the table and stared at the white-coated scene outside. "It doesn't look too deep to me. Besides, I rented an SUV."

"I know." She picked up a carving knife and hacked at the slightly stale bagel she'd found in the bread bin. "It was a good idea, too."

"It's for driving in the snow."

"It's for driving without chains on snowy pavement that's been plowed." She glanced over her shoulder at him. "I'm not sure a city slicker like you could handle an off-road, cross-country trek."

"Are you saying we might be stuck here?" He cleared his throat, neatly covering the note of panic she'd heard in his voice. "Isn't there someone we can call?"

"About what?"

"About getting us out of here."

"You just got here." She turned with a smile and offered half the bagel, slathered with cream cheese. "Relax. It's Saturday. Put your feet up. Have a bagel."

"I don't want a bagel. Thank you," he added politely. "I'd like to see about arranging for an Internet connection."

"Ah, yes. The Internet. First things first."

"I do have work to do."

Somewhere in that briefcase was a job offer she wasn't ready to consider and paperwork she dreaded reading. She pasted on a brilliant smile and cocked her head to one side, prepared to deal with things as best she could. "What kind of work, exactly?"

"My job."

She lifted an eyebrow and bit into the bagel. "Excuse me for prying."

He sighed and pinched the bridge of his nose. "And excuse me for snapping at you. I guess I need some coffee."

"Me, too." She shrugged. "I didn't remember that I'm out, or I'd have borrowed some from Jenna last night."

"You don't have any coffee?"

"Nope."

"Tea?"

"Sorry. Finished that off last night."

"Juice?"

"Apple."

"I'll take it," he said. "Unless you need it. For the baby."

"Ashley doesn't drink apple juice."

"I meant…" A charming blush stained his cheeks. "Where is she, by the way?"

"Napping."

"In the morning?"

"She naps through the day, off and on." Nora opened the refrigerator door and pulled a bottle of juice from one of the shelves. "You learn to cram all the nonbaby activities into the quiet times."

She took a glass from one of the honey-toned oak cupboards and filled it with juice. "We're not really trapped here, you know."

"We're not?"

"Will's coming by. He called while you were in the shower. If he can make it in, we can make it out."

"How's he getting here?"

"On horseback." She couldn't resist teasing him. He was so cute when he went all pale and shocky. "Maybe. But he'll probably drive his big ranch truck."

"And will he have coffee?" Burke asked as she handed him the glass.

"I think he mentioned something about Jenna sending a Thermos with him."

"Thank God," said Burke.

"Sure you don't want the other half of this?" Nora asked around a mouthful of bagel.

"No. Thank you. I'll wait for the coffee."

"It's going to be a long time until lunch."

"What are we having?"

Nora shot him a wicked smile. "The rest of the apple juice."

He narrowed his eyes at her. "There's a grocery store in Tucker."

"Yes, I know." She took another bite of her breakfast. "Jenna and I go shopping there together at least once a week."

"I could take you."

She nodded, looking forward to a trip into town. "We could make a morning of it, get everything we need. I want to pick up some more diapers while we're at it."

We could do this, *we* could do that. More impulsive plans.

He lifted his briefcase and then paused with a frown before nudging aside Ashley's plastic key ring and pink squishy doll to make a space on one side of the table. He opened the case and pulled out a yellow pad of paper and a slender pen, and then paused to prop the doll against the case when it threatened to topple facedown on the paper.

Once he had the doll's posture under control, he arranged his office supplies with crisp, practiced moves, aligning the pad with the end of the table and placing the shiny pen precisely one inch from the right margin.

"What are you doing?" asked Nora.

"Making a list."

"For the grocery store?" She bit back a smile as he clicked his pen and printed some sort of heading in tidy block letters across the top of the notepad. "I thought we'd just wander up and down the aisles, figure out what we need and toss it into the cart."

His frown deepened as he started a second column. "You mentioned diapers."

"I won't forget those."

"You might forget the coffee again."

"If I do, you'll remember."

"Right. Because I'm writing it down."

He'd already added several items to his neat list, a determined set to his jaw and a slight wrinkle between his brows. As he worked, a thick hunk of drying hair slipped forward over his forehead, brushing the rim of his glasses.

God, he was appealing when he was being anal. Downright kissable.

Kissable? Burke?

She stuffed the rest of the bagel into her mouth and fled to her room to change. A visit to town was a good idea. She definitely needed to get out more.

BURKE FINISHED the first draft of the errands list—outlined in order of priority, according to the locations they needed to visit and the items that required refrigeration—and stood to stretch the kinks from his back. Yesterday's travel and last night's overly firm mattress had left him stiff and achy. A stroll through Tucker would loosen the knots and help sharpen his focus.

He needed to prioritize, to concentrate and regroup. This place and Nora's presence—and her baby—were playing havoc with his systematic methods of achieving a goal. Even the view out the window was a potent distraction: the dramatic sweep of diamond-white fields, the silver tracery of bare tree limbs twined with the black ribbon of the creek, the ice-etched mountains that punched into the sapphire bowl of the sky with rough-knuckled power.

To help get some of that focus back, he turned his sore back on the beauty outside to face the runner-up view of the cabin's untidy front room. A nondescript tweed sofa and an oversized rocker formed the seating area near the porch door, and a rickety dining table with three chairs—one of them missing a back slat—were arranged in the open end of the L-shaped kitchen. Baby toys in garish colors were strewn across the center of a wrinkled blanket on the floor and littered several tabletops and chair seats.

The contrast with Nora's elegant place in the Hollywood Hills was so extreme he couldn't understand how she could spend more than a day here without looking for a means of escape. And yet he could see the evidence of her attempts to settle in and make it her own—the lively patterns and vivid colors he remembered from her sample books. A Provençal-print pillow tossed on the rocker's seat, a cluster of jewel-bright bottles gathering dust on the windowsill, a checkered throw draped carelessly over one arm of the sofa. Flowers wilted in a fat blue-and-white pitcher on the kitchen counter and a red ceramic rooster struck an arrogant pose near a sink stacked with dirty dishes.

The idea of Nora trying to cope with the housekeeping chores didn't bother him nearly as much as the image of her adding those homey touches.

He nudged a chunky four-note xylophone aside with his foot, wondering if she missed her piano. She'd sometimes entertained her guests with the music she'd make in the niche near her solarium, with the sunlight streaming in through the tall, arched windows behind her and the scents of gardenia and citrus wafting through the air with the notes. Mozart, Schumann, Porter and Gershwin. He'd missed settling into one of the wicker chairs in the corner, partially hidden beneath the feathery ferns spilling over their tall stands, listening to the rich sounds and her smoky laughter.

A flash of sunlight on chrome caught his attention, and he turned to see Will's truck lumber up the short rise toward the cabin porch, trailing clods of snow and a thick white cloud of exhaust. He slid down from the cab, a hat pulled low over his face and the collar of a thick jacket flipped up to meet the brim, a Thermos in one hand and a newspaper in the other.

Room service, ranch-style.

Burke stepped out the front door and gasped as the wicked chill stung through his thinly layered clothing. He'd have to add a new word to his vocabulary to describe the sensation of being freeze-dried without the dignity of airtight plastic packaging.

"Beautiful day," said Will with a nod.

Since he was avoiding inhaling another lungful of icy air to respond to the comment, Burke simply nodded back.

"A might nippy," said the foreman as he passed Burke and headed into the cabin's front room, "but a shame to spend it cooped up inside."

A shame to spend a day like this anywhere but on a beach in California.

Will dropped the paper on the table beside Burke's laptop and pulled three mugs from one of the cupboards. He poured steaming coffee into one of them. "I figure you might be kind of anxious for some of this by now."

"You figured correctly. Thanks," said Burke as the foreman handed him a mug. "Jenna's coffee is worth waiting for."

"She's got a gift for cooking." Will filled a second mug to toast his wife's talents. "One of the many reasons I was so bent on marrying her."

He took a sip, leaned against the counter and crossed his legs at the ankles. "I'll be heading into Sheridan this morning after I check in with the ranch crew. Should have a new water heater working for you by dinnertime."

Burke glanced at the rooster. "No need to hurry. If Nora's willing to put up with me for another day or two, I don't mind staying here."

Will sipped his coffee and subjected Burke to squinty-eyed scrutiny over the rim of his mug. "I guess we'll leave it up to her, then."

Nora entered the room, Ashley in her arms and a gigantic black bag dangling from a thick shoulder strap. The baby was bundled into a bright pink sweatshirt with a fuzzy ball attached to the pointed hood and wrapped in a thick blanket. "Hey, Will."

"Hey, Nora." He set down his coffee and held out his arms for the baby. "Hey, sweet pea. Look at you, all bundled up. Going somewhere?"

"We're heading into Tucker for some supplies." Nora picked up the Thermos. "Jenna need anything?"

"Supplies, eh?" Will gave Burke another of those long, considering looks as he settled the baby in the crook of one arm. "You could give her a call, I s'pose."

"I will." Nora sipped her coffee. "Maybe she'd like to go with us."

She gazed expectantly at Burke, but he didn't offer to include Jenna in their outing. He'd hoped to use the time alone with Nora to lay the groundwork for the business he needed to discuss with her. "There are a few things I need besides groceries," he said. "We may be gone quite a while."

"Then we can have lunch in town."

"If you'd like."

"Now, that sounds like a fine idea," said Will. "Loretta at the Beaverhead's been complaining how she hasn't seen little Miss Ashley here in the longest time."

The Beaverhead. Burke remembered his one visit to the diner during the shoot last summer. And the case of heartburn that had followed.

"We'll have to stop by, then," said Nora. "Won't we, Ashley?"

The baby responded by emitting a stream of white goo over her chin and sweatshirt front. Will plucked the cloth from Nora's shoulder and swiped at the worst of it, and then glanced at Burke. "I don't s'pose you'd be interested in swinging by the calving barn later this afternoon, getting a firsthand look at some ranch work while you're here."

Burke frowned. "I'm afraid I have work of my own to do."

"I s'pose you do. And plenty of it, I imagine." The foreman's squint deepened with the hint of a smile. "Just thought you might like to take a different kind of break, see some different sights you don't get to see too often out in your part of the world."

Burke hoped he hadn't appeared ungrateful for the invitation. "You're right. I should make the most of the opportunity. I'll see if I can fit it into my schedule."

"Schedule." One corner of Will's mouth quirked in a lopsided grin. "Sounds mighty important the way you put it. Wouldn't want to interfere."

"Are you still pulling calves?" asked Nora.

"We pull 'em pretty much round the clock this time of year." He handed Ashley back and scrubbed at some goo stuck to his jacket front. "No need to make up your mind about it now. You know where you can find me."

He lifted his hand to the front of his hat brim, murmured a folksy farewell to Burke and "the ladies" and ducked out the door.

"Pulling calves?" Burke raised one eyebrow at Nora. "I don't suppose that's anything like pulling taffy?"

"You'll find out." She tsked over the stain on Ashley's front. "I think I'm going to change her jacket. A lady always wants to look her best when she makes her entrance."

Burke didn't see the point in trading one outfit for another, unless the next one featured a king-sized, waterproof lobster bib.

"In fact," she continued, "I think I'll dash on a bit of lipstick. Maybe change into my best pair of jeans. Better get your jacket," she said as she headed toward the hall. "Just because the sun's out doesn't mean it's going to warm up today."

"Does it ever warm up?"

"It's warm in the calving barn."

She aimed another pleading look in his direction, and he didn't have the heart to disappoint her again, not after ignoring her unspoken request to include Jenna in their outing. Chances were he wouldn't find what he needed in Tucker or be able to make the necessary business arrangements on a Saturday, anyway. He might as well spend the day in a casual visit, laying a bit of groundwork for a fruitful discussion.

"Then I definitely want to see it," he said.

"Who knows, you might even enjoy it."

He didn't think it was possible to enjoy anything found in a barn, but he pasted on a cheerful smile and went to his room to dress for several hours of freezing temperatures, Montana-style marketing, heartburn-inducing food and livestock viewing.

All in a day's work.

CHAPTER SIX

"HEY, NORA."

"Hey, Brenda. Heard your husband broke his ankle."

Burke bit back a sigh as Nora struck up yet another conversation with yet another stranger who'd happened to wander into the same aisle at the market. He'd already waited through a dozen conversations in the pharmacy and another dozen at the bakery. The chatty lunchtime group in the Beaverhead would have constituted a standing-room-only audience in a small theater just off Sunset.

And Nora always had enjoyed working a crowd.

He'd had to admit, as he'd watched her gasp and nod over the gossip, as she'd frowned and groaned over a bit of bad news, as she'd very nearly glowed over compliments for Ashley, that he couldn't remember the last time he'd seen her looking so bright and animated. Her last months in Hollywood had been stressful and exhausting as she struggled through her studio work while dealing with a difficult pregnancy and a painful divorce. He couldn't blame her for escaping to the relative peace of Fitz's ranch at her first chance.

And he hadn't seen her this delighted over so many things—so many simple, basic, down-to-earth things—in a long while. Maybe never, now that he thought about it. He disliked the conclusion he'd reached, but it appeared that life in Tucker agreed with her. The people here had taken her in with the kind of casual acceptance a celebrity couldn't help but crave.

Yet though he'd always suspected she could pull off the chameleon stunt better than anyone he knew—with the possible exception of Fitz Kelleran—he was still surprised she'd chosen to expend so much time and energy adapting to this place and these people. She was the kind of woman who should spend her Saturday morning getting a facial or window-shopping on Rodeo Drive, not trekking through the snow for a loaf of sourdough. Someone with her talent and beauty should be considering her next film role, not choosing a brand of bottled marinara sauce.

He nodded and stepped aside as another customer wandered past. Tucker claimed only a few hundred residents, but it seemed the entire population had decided to do their shopping today, and all of them had to say hey to each other and stop to trade mind-numbingly dull opinions about the weather, or the freshly painted boxes at the post office, or the new traffic signal at the end of Main Street or the number of elk in the foothills. Or the exact amount of pasta to add to a pot of boiling water to make two portions of spaghetti.

"You won't forget, will you, Burke?"

Nora waited for his reply, and he realized he'd drifted dangerously close to a near-vegetative state—brought on, no doubt, by staring at the same row of canned vegetables for the past half hour.

"About the pasta?" he asked.

Her smile told him he'd managed to snap out of his stupor and land in the correct place in the conversation. "Not if I want to eat," he said.

"I never follow the cooking times listed on the package, though," said Brenda. "It always seems a touch undercooked when I do."

"Al dente," Burke murmured.

"Al-what?"

"Stick-to-your-teeth," he said. "It's an Italian term."

The two women stared at him. Another minor eruption of curdled goo oozed from Ashley's mouth and dripped along the front of a pretty blue jacket dotted with tiny chicks. Or ducks.

Something small and yellow, at any rate.

"I don't know much about that Eye-talian style of cooking," said Brenda. "Stick-to-your-ribs is what I'm after."

Burke ducked out of the conversation to take the cloth draped over the side of the stroller and clean the baby's face. If he didn't get out of this store, someone might soon be wiping drool from his chin, too.

"Brenda, did you meet Burke when he was here for the film shoot last summer?"

"I don't believe I did."

"Burke." Nora tugged at his arm, and he straightened with a polite smile pasted in place. "This is Brenda Moseley."

"How do you do, Brenda?"

"Just fine, thank you." Brenda's smile was sharp and calculating. "Aren't you the fella who worked for Fitz? His personal trainer?"

"Personal assistant."

Brenda waved away the distinction. "I can't keep all that personal this-and-that stuff straight. "

"This-and-that can be confusing at times," said Burke.

"Burke's a producer now." Nora squeezed his arm a bit, probably warning him to be on his best behavior. "He's helping Fitz with his newest project."

"Isn't that interesting?"

"Utterly absorbing," he said. "I should move along now, so I can devote some time today to working on it."

Nora's grip tightened in a nasty pinch before she released his arm. "We weren't able to get everything Burke needs. Too bad Ellison's Office Supplies was closed today."

"The note on the door says Sam's at his sister's in Billings," said Brenda with another sharklike smile, "but rumor has it he went to Dillon to pay a social call on a certain lady friend."

"*Really?*" asked Nora breathlessly.

"Sam Ellison?" Burke had met the dour, ancient man last summer while shopping for Jody's birthday present. "He doesn't seem the 'social call' type."

The two women stared at him again, and he realized with hot-faced horror that he'd been sucked into the maw of Tucker gossip.

"Well, we'd better go," said Nora with an apologetic smile. "It's always nice seeing you, Brenda. Please tell Jim I said hello."

She pushed the stroller around the corner and paused to examine a bag of cat food.

"What are you doing?" she whispered when Burke stopped beside her.

"What are *you* doing?" He consulted the paper in his hand. "Cat food's not on the list."

"Why did you talk to Brenda like that?"

"Like what?"

"You made it seem like your business was more important than visiting with her. And what was that crack about Sam?"

A dozen responses came to mind—logical, reasonable points that obviously needed to be made—but none of them seemed worth the trouble they'd cause, so he kept his mouth shut.

"You can't do that with Brenda." Nora sighed and shoved at her hair. "She's got the biggest mouth in town. She'll tell everyone what you said."

"What? That I eat my pasta raw?"

She clapped a hand over her mouth. Above

her fingers, her dark eyes gleamed with amusement and a spark or two of the old scandal-raising fire.

It was the first time since her divorce that he'd seen a glimpse of the Nora he used to know, the one who'd lived life as if it had no limits. The one he'd fussed and worried over, the one he'd missed. Something seemed to break loose inside him and bubble up, spreading a smile across his face, making him warm and light-headed all at once.

He waited until Brenda's cart edged around the aisle at the other end, and then he boxed Nora in against the cat food and leaned close to give Brenda something to gossip over at her next stop. "Come on, Nora," he whispered in her ear. "Let's live dangerously and follow the package cooking instructions."

She gave him one of her smokiest glances, the one that flickered from beneath her thick, sooty lashes. "Exactly as written?"

"Precisely."

He stepped back and nodded at Brenda as she passed them. "Thanks again for the cooking tip."

"HEY, NORA." Dusty McLane, the sheriff's deputy, strode down the sidewalk toward

Burke's parking spot outside North Town Market.

"Hey, Dusty." Nora caught the beginning of one of Burke's long-suffering sighs before he ducked into the car to place another grocery sack near Ashley's car seat. Though he must have been excruciatingly bored, he'd managed to remain pleasant enough through most of her socializing. But even Burke's amazing supply of patience had its limits.

"How's it going?" she asked Dusty.

"Can't complain. Is that Ashley?" He leaned toward the stroller and gave the baby's foot a friendly pinch. "Is that my pretty girl? How old are you now?"

"Nearly four months."

"And looking more like your mama every day." He glanced over his shoulder with one of his charming, crooked grins. "Can I hold her for you while you pack up her stroller in the car?"

"Thanks, Dusty." Nora reached down to unfasten the stroller's harness, but Dusty flicked through the series of plastic latches with no trouble.

"There's my girl." He lifted her smoothly into his arms and wrapped the blanket around her legs. "Remember me, sweetheart? How's about a smile?"

Nora watched in amazement as Ashley bestowed one of her rare gummy grins on the soft-spoken man. Smiling was one of her newest tricks, and she rarely practiced it with anyone but Nora and Jenna.

"Well, look at that," he said as he brushed a fingertip down the baby's cheek. "You flirt just like your mama, too."

"I don't flirt."

"Now, there's a pity." His gaze drifted down to Nora's mouth and back up again. "But a guy like me can always hope you'll mend your ways."

It was the first time since she'd set her divorce in motion, since she'd grown clumsy with pregnancy and given birth, that a man had looked at her with heat in his eyes. The unexpected warmth tugged at her like sunshine drawing a spring seedling from the cold, bare ground.

He walked with Ashley toward the display window of Hanson's Pet Store. "Just look at those kittens, sweetheart. I bet someday you'll be wanting one of those, won't you?"

Nora followed him. "Don't give her any ideas."

"Nothing wrong with a kitten in a little girl's life, at the right time." He rubbed his cheek against the side of Ashley's jacket hood. "A girl's gotta have something to love."

"I heard you were a sweet-talking man, Dusty McLane." Nora narrowed her eyes at him when his grin widened. "But I had no idea how good you were at it."

"Darlin', I'm willing to show you exactly how good I can be, any time."

Yes, he probably was willing. There might be plenty of single men in Montana who'd be willing to offer her much, much more than sweet-talking. But if she chose to settle down with one of them, would he resent her need to travel to California or New York for work? And did she want to live her life in two locations? Did she want to be separated from her daughter, or separate her daughter from one life or another for long stretches of time?

Was she ready to make a clean break with her past life and start a new one?

She didn't have to decide today. Today she would simply soak up the sunshine.

She followed Ashley's lead and gave Dusty one of her best smiles. "That's a mighty tempting offer."

He shifted the baby to his shoulder. "Nothing wrong with a little temptation in a girl's life, either."

AFTER LOADING the last of the grocery sacks and pushing the market cart into its parking spot, Burke found Nora on the sidewalk, continuing her visit with the tall, lanky cowpoke dressed in the local cold weather uniform of wide-brimmed hat, bulky jacket and worn jeans. The man cradled Ashley in his arms, rocking slightly from side to side on his boot heels.

Probably another ten-minute discussion of a two-minute topic.

Looking for an excuse to avoid another conversation about something as scintillating as winter feed, he confronted Ashley's stroller and, after pressing a dozen buttons and levers, managed to wrestle it into a smaller, flatter version. He opened the rear compartment of his rental car and made a spot for the stroller beside the bulging diaper case, the waste container filled with soiled diapers, the two bargain-sized bags of new diapers, the plastic carton filled with travel toys, the bag of bakery goods and the blankets and emergency supplies Will suggested he carry with him, and closed the door. When he'd rented the cavernous SUV two days ago, he'd never imagined he'd worry about running out of space.

The phone in his pocket buzzed, and after another glance in Nora's direction he moved to the passenger side of the car for a bit of privacy. "Burke Elliot here."

"Hey, Burke."

"I suppose I'm expected to respond to that by saying 'Hey, Fitz.'"

"Nah. It doesn't sound right when you do it."

"I'm glad to hear it. That will relieve me of a small degree of social pressure while I'm here."

"Pressure? You're practically on vacation."

"It's that 'practically' part that trips me up, every time." He shifted to check on Nora, who seemed to be engrossed in a storefront window display. "Why are you calling?"

"Just checking in. Heard about the problem with the water heater. Sorry about that."

"So was I, at first. But it gave me a chance for a private visit with Nora after dinner."

"Jenna told me Nora put you up at her

place." Fitz paused. "And Ellie says Jenna wasn't too happy about it."

Nora smiled and curled her fingers in a little wave. He returned the gesture and then turned his back on her and her friend. "I wonder why you bothered to check in with me," he told Fitz. "Your spies have already given you a full report."

"What's the matter, the cold getting to you?"

"It already got to me. I'm numb from the top of my unfashionably capped head to my nonexistent toes."

"You can defrost when you get back." Fitz mumbled something to someone on his end. "Are you going to have a chance for another private visit with her today, do you think?"

"Later, perhaps, when we're in the car heading back to the ranch. We're in town right now, collecting a few things we need. But I'm sure you already knew that, too."

He heard Nora's laughter and turned to see the cowboy lean in close, his hat brim nearly brushing her hair. Burke narrowed his eyes. "It all depends on whether the baby decides to scream all the way back to the cabin."

"Screamin' Mimi. She's sure got a set of lungs on her, doesn't she?"

"They seem to be in perfect working order." Unlike her digestive system.

"Excuse me for a minute." Fitz's voice was muffled and indistinct as he discussed something with someone on the other end.

Who was that man putting his hand on Nora's arm? And why was she tilting her head in full flirting mode to listen to what he was saying?

"I'd better get going," said Fitz. "Just wanted you to know that the fact you're out there seems to have satisfied Greenberg, for the moment at any rate. But he's going to start looking for results in another day or two."

"And if she refuses?"

"She won't."

She laughed again, tossing her hair back with a casual shake of her head and looking up at the cowpoke with her wide-eyed, innocent-schoolgirl expression.

Burke recognized those moves. There was nothing casual or innocent about them.

He dragged his gaze from the cozy scene and focused on business. "She refused you."

"That's probably 'cause I didn't ask her the right way."

Burke's fingers tightened around the phone. "Did you ask her at all?"

Fitz paused. "Not in so many words."

"Yes or no, Fitz."

"It's not that simple. But I'm sure she got the basic idea."

"You sent me all the way out here to ask Nora a question you could have asked her yourself?"

"I laid all the groundwork. See how easy I made this for you?"

"Fitz—"

"Gotta run. Bye." *Click.*

Burke stared at the phone. "Damn."

Nora stepped to his side. Above the baby fussing in her arms, her cheeks were flushed and her eyes seemed to sparkle. "Everything okay?"

"Everything's fine, just fine." He slid the phone into his pocket. "Practically perfect."

CHAPTER SEVEN

NORA STARED at Burke's frowning profile as he drove toward Granite Ridge. She wondered if he was preparing to launch the contract discussion she knew was coming, but then she decided he'd wait for a more businesslike setting. "Was that Fitz on the phone?" she asked.

"Yes."

"I can always tell when it's Fitz. You get this little crease right in the middle of your forehead." She leaned toward him and playfully traced the spot.

"I wouldn't do that if I were you. That crease means my blood pressure is shoving all the tissue in my head into position for detonation."

"You know you love it." She twisted in her seat to check on Ashley, who was busy blowing a baby raspberry. "You love him, too."

"It's a rare form of mental illness." He

slowed to make a careful turn on a snowy stretch of road. "I used to think it was a case of possession, and I arranged for an exorcism. But the witch doctor ran screaming from the room."

Nora laughed and stared out the window, reveling in the moment along with the scenery, enjoying one of those intensely crystalline days she'd never known in the hazy city atmospheres of Los Angeles and New York. The jutting shards of the mountains, the frozen waterfall of a naked willow, the black gash of a fence post—the brilliant sun seemed to charge things with energy, to touch them with secret fire, to heighten the contrasts of light and shade and deepen the colors.

Flashing lights, inky tuxedos, abstract dashes of jewel-toned couture. A year ago she'd been riding in a limousine, on her way to a gala premiere, her handsome husband seated beside her, the silk and froth of a Valentino gown swirled about her feet and a fortune in borrowed diamonds draped about her throat. Today the scents of baby and wool and laundry detergent, the soft hum of the pavement and the papery rustle of grocery packages were no less capable of giving her the same sense of satisfaction.

As another mile slipped past in silence, she became aware of how relaxed she felt, how comfortable she could be with Burke. She hadn't been certain, at first, that she could tolerate a steady dose of his moodiness, but she was beginning to understand he wasn't nearly as stiff and grouchy as he appeared to be. And she suspected he used that formal and faintly disapproving air as a shield to maintain his privacy, as a way to salvage some small degree of personal order and control in the midst of the chaos that usually surrounded him.

Her theory helped explain why Fitz had ignored Burke's wet-blanket routine all these years. She'd decided to shrug it off, too. Easy to do, since she also found it oddly endearing.

Behind them, Ashley kicked her feet restlessly and squawked. Burke's hands tightened on the steering wheel, and his brow folded in another crease.

"Relax," said Nora. "She's not working up to a fit. That's just her way of talking."

"She needs to work on her inflection."

When Ashley quieted again, he eased his grip and exhaled with obvious relief. "I was afraid her stomach might be bothering her."

"Don't worry." Nora reached back to shove Ashley's pacifier back into her mouth.

"After you've spent more time with her, you'll learn to tell the difference. Inflection and all."

As she turned to face front again, she caught Burke staring at her. The frown line in his forehead was deeper than ever.

"Who was the man on the sidewalk?" he asked.

"Which man?"

"The one on the sidewalk, outside the market. The one who pulled Ashley from her stroller."

"Dusty McClane. The sheriff's deputy."

Burke made the turn into Granite Ridge, and they bumped across the first cattle guard. "You seemed to know him rather well."

"Not really."

"He seems to like Ashley."

"Most people do," she pointed out.

"He seems to like her a bit more than most."

"Why are you so concerned with how much Dusty likes Ashley?"

He had no answer for her, and she stared at him with a knowing grin. "You're not concerned about Ashley. You're jealous of Dusty and me."

"Of you and Dusty?" Burke slowed the car to a crawl. "Why would I be?"

"I have no idea. Why would you be?"

"Well, I'm not."

"I know you're not jealous on Ashley's behalf." Nora folded her arms across her chest with a sigh. "I'm still not convinced you like her."

"I don't dislike her," he said after a slight pause.

"But you don't *like* her."

"I don't know her well enough yet to know whether I like her or not."

"She's a baby." Nora shook her head in amazement. "What do you have to know about a baby?"

"I don't know. That's the point, I suppose." He moved his shoulders in something resembling a shrug, and a blush darkened his cheeks. "She's the first baby I've ever met."

"She is?"

He coasted to a stop near the fence and shifted to face her. "I don't know what to do with a baby. How to feel about it—her. How I'm supposed to feel. I didn't know what to expect, but I didn't think it would be…this," he said at last, turning to gaze out the windshield. "It's not that I don't like her, Nora, it's just that I don't—I don't know what to do for her. How to relate to her, how to communicate with her."

"You don't have to relate to her. You just have to like her. To love her, if you can."

"But she—she won't love me back."

"Does it matter?"

He gave her a long, shuttered look. A look that tugged at her on a different, deeper level than Dusty's sweet-talking.

"No," he said at last, "I don't suppose it does."

HAD IT ONLY BEEN a couple of hours since she'd coasted along the road, smugly enjoying her life?

Nora shifted an inconsolable Ashley higher on her shoulder and stirred the bubbling red sauce. Steam from the water simmering on the next burner teased strands of her hair from its loosening clasp and curled it around her eyes, adding to her irritation.

She probably looked exactly the way she felt: a wreck.

No matter how bad she looked, it was nothing compared to the kitchen. The sauce had spewed a greasy red mist around the burner, a smear of garlic spread coated a corner of the crumb-covered chopping board and dishes from this morning had been shoved aside in an untidy mess. Why hadn't she accepted Jenna's dinner invitation? Burke probably would have preferred pot roast with all the trimmings to spaghetti with prepackaged salad and garlic bread.

And no dessert. *"Damn."*

After he'd helped store the groceries, tolerated another exuberant welcome from a nipping Rowdy and survived the horrors of the calving barn, Burke had taken the cabin's phone and shut himself away in his room to make some calls. At the time, Nora had been delighted to have a brief break in the constant social interaction. But now she wished he'd come out of hiding and give her a hand with the dinner preparations.

Not that his efforts would be all that much help. She was aware that Fitz had started feeding Burke after discovering his meals consisted of things that could be toasted, microwaved, eaten raw or packaged in take-out containers. And Burke had demonstrated his appreciation by eating every gourmet dish the actor whipped up and set in front of him.

Nora wished Fitz were here tonight to nudge her aside and make everything wonderful. Since he wasn't, the most she could hope for was edible. Jenna had taught her a few—a very few—cooking skills during the past months, but she was still far from competent in the kitchen.

Tonight's dinner was part of her campaign to prove she could manage a simpler lifestyle on her own. Just as all her frantic socializing in Tucker had demonstrated how delighted she could be with a life in Montana.

She hoped Burke would get the message, pack his briefcase and go back to California, where he belonged—tomorrow, if possible. Keeping up the act this long was exhausting.

Ashley scrunched into a clinging ball of misery and howled again, and Nora dropped the spoon to rub her back. "Shh," she said, though she knew it was useless. The active day had upset the baby's schedule and left her fussier than usual. "Shh, sweetie, it's all right."

"Is there something I can do?"

Nora turned to see Burke standing in the middle of the room, looking competent and uncertain all at once. "Yes," she said. "You can hold Ashley while I dump the noodles in the water."

He took a moment to adjust his glasses—his version of girding for battle—and then covered his shoulder with a cloth diaper before clumsily taking the baby into his arms.

"We're having spaghetti, and a salad and—"

The bread. Nora opened the oven door, and a cloud of black smoke stung her eyes. "And no bread."

"That's all right. I've decided to cut back on carbs."

"Stop being so agreeable." She waved at the smoke. "It's a disaster."

"Another one, anyway."

She glanced over her shoulder to see Burke pluck gingerly at his shirt and frown at a dark splotch. Ashley's diaper hadn't done its job. "That's not a disaster."

"All right." He shifted the whimpering baby as far from his body as he could manage. "I'll downgrade my assessment from a disaster to an extremely unpleasant experience. Somewhere on a scale between being mugged by that brown dog and watching Will shove his arm inside a cow's bottom."

She laughed and grabbed an oven mitt to pull the bread from the oven. *"Ow."*

The pan clattered to the floor.

Hopping over scattered bread slices, she

rushed to the sink to run cold water over her burned thumb. "You'll have to change it, then."

"Change what?"

"The diaper."

"Me?"

"Yes, you." She huffed in exasperation at the curls hanging in her eyes. "Unless you want to take over here."

He cast a worried look at the water bubbling over the sides of the pot to hiss against the burner and then marched into the kitchen like a condemned man. "Tell me what to do."

"See if the noodles are finished cooking, and if they are, dump them in the colander."

"What colander?"

She rummaged through the cupboards. "I know I put it in here somewhere."

"I'll find it." He passed a squirming Ashley to Nora. "How will I know if the noodles are done?"

"Hey, you're the al dente man."

She hugged the baby close and nuzzled her neck, unconcerned about the leaking diaper. The solid little body felt so good against hers, and one more mess wouldn't matter.

"I'm sorry, Burke," she said with a sigh. "I thought I could handle this."

"It's all right. I thought I could be more help."

He straightened his glasses and gave her an apologetic smile. There he stood, smudged with filth, charred bread at his feet and a red splatter pattern at his back, taking on more than his fair share.

Her hero.

She went up on her toes to peck at his cheek. "How about those noodles?"

He examined the limp, bloated pasta he fished out of the water. "How about a pizza?"

"They don't deliver," she called over her shoulder as she headed down the hall toward her room.

A few moments later, he appeared in the doorway. "I could go into town and pick one up."

"Ashley and I'll come with you."

"I wasn't planning on coming back."

She laughed again, delighted with the way his serious expression somehow lightened the situation. "I don't blame you."

He remained in place, watching her unfasten the snaps near Ashley's crotch.

"Have you ever changed a diaper?" she asked.

"No."

"It's not that hard." She removed the soiled outfit and pitched it into the nearby hamper.

"I'll take your word for it."

"Come here." She stepped to the side and waited until he heaved one of his long-suffering sighs and entered the room. "See how it's fastened? With tape?"

"Mmm-hmm."

She peeled back the tape and pulled the diaper open.

"Oh, my God," he said.

Nora had seen worse, but she supposed this mess may have been a bit traumatic for a first-timer. With a few practiced moves, she wiped Ashley clean with several disposable cloths.

"Okay, I've done the hard part," she said, extending a fresh diaper in his direction. "You do the rest."

"Must I?"

"Yes."

"May I ask why?"

She lifted one of his hands and slapped the diaper into it. "I'm going to freshen up for the trip into town. You're on your own for the next few minutes."

"What if I do it wrong?"

"I'll check when I'm finished." She pulled

a blanket-weight pajama outfit from a dresser drawer below the changing pad and shoved it into his other hand. "Whatever you do, don't turn your back on her, not for one second. She hasn't tried anything yet, but you wouldn't want her to roll off the changing table and fall on the floor."

The look of horror on his face assured her Ashley was in safe hands.

CHAPTER EIGHT

BURKE WONDERED if babies blushed. His own face was hot as he undid the tapes on the contraption Nora had given him. He'd viewed the naked female form before—on several occasions, on several different naked females—but the forms he'd seen had been…different. More mature. And capable of deciding for themselves whether or not to let a strange man have a look at them.

Not that he wanted to look. But he had to look somewhere if he was going to get the diaper where it needed to go.

"I beg your pardon," he said.

Ashley studied him, a solemn look on her chubby face but not a sign of a blush in sight. She poked one of her fingers into her mouth and sucked noisily for a second, and then pushed it in farther until she gagged. A thin line of curd-flecked drool slid across her cheek and dripped on the pad beneath her.

"What did you think would happen if you did that, hmm?" He set the nappy and pajamas to one side, placed a hand over the baby's stomach to prevent her from plummeting to the floor and stretched toward one of the cloths hanging over the edge of the crib. "Well, now you know. See that it doesn't happen again."

The cloth was out of reach. Behind him, he heard the soft plop of the nappy falling to the floor.

"Damn. Sorry—*darn*."

He turned to find a puddle spreading below the baby's bottom.

"*What the—*" He grasped her by the ankles the way Nora had done and lifted her to sop at the wet with the first thing he could grab.

Her pajamas.

The pajamas he was supposed to have dressed her in. After he'd put on the diaper that would have prevented this latest disaster.

"It's not a disaster," he muttered as he tossed the pajamas into the hamper. He gathered a handful of disposable wipes and scrubbed a bit at the cushioned pad and Ashley's lower back. "It's another bloody unpleasant situation."

He wiped his own hands, too, and dabbed the drool from the baby's chin before confronting the nappy again. He'd forgotten already—were the tapes supposed to face up or down?

"I don't suppose you could give me a hint?"

Her lower lip plumped in a miniature pout, and she began to whimper.

"You're getting cold, aren't you?" He snatched at her ankles and shoved the diaper beneath her, and then retrieved it to fan it open and try a second time to position it correctly. "I'm hurrying as fast as I can."

She arched her back and rolled to her side.

"Come back here," he begged, grasping her tiny, tender shoulder. "This way. Right now. *Please.*"

He gently guided her to her back and grasped the tapes, hoping he wasn't fastening the diaper too tightly. Or too loosely. Or backward.

Whatever he did, Nora would make it right. She'd said she'd check his work, hadn't she?

The baby did her best to make things difficult, raising her knees and bumping his hands out of range. "Come on, Ashley, there's a good girl. *Stop it.*"

She stilled and stared at him, and he held

his breath, bracing for the squawks and the crying jag he was certain would follow. His heartbeats thundered in his ears.

The crisis passed. Coronary averted.

He yanked open the drawer and found dozens of outfits. Or, more correctly, pieces of outfits. White leggings and printed T-shirts, pink sweaters and frilly bloomers. A second drawer was filled with nappies and cloth squares like the ones dangling over the crib.

Nothing that resembled the cozy pajamas he'd panicked and used for a rag.

"Blank. Blank. *Blank.*"

WAA-UH-WAAAAAAH.

"God." Burke opened one eye in a blurry slit to check the glowing green numbers on his bedside clock screen—2:17 a.m. In the morning, of course.

Waa-uh-uh-waah.

His stomach knotted in sympathy. Poor little girl. Poor, poor Ashley. How awful it must be to suffer without understanding why, without knowing the pain would pass. How wearying it must be for Nora to be unable to offer any relief, to endure the heart-twisting crying and the sleepless hours, night after night.

How could she endure it? He hadn't

realized there was a core of steel beneath that vivacious exterior.

He hadn't had to deal with the reality of an infant, hadn't had to carry the awesome responsibility for that small, helpless person for more than a few minutes at a time, and—

Waaaaah.

Thank God.

He rolled to his back and flung an arm across his eyes. Had he ever been this exhausted? What about that day he'd come down with the flu during a charity jog-a-thon? Or the time he'd pulled a nonstop shift during that crazy stint in Cannes? No. Not even Fitz's weekend-long celebration of his Golden Globe nomination had worn him down like this.

An entire day, a miserable, endless, tooth-ache of a day spent in this godforsaken place, and he was no closer to closing this deal and making his escape. Nora's contract lay untouched in his briefcase.

Damn.

But there had been that dinner at Walt's Burgers late last night. Joint by joint, nerve by nerve, he'd relaxed in a comfortable sprawl as Ashley'd snoozed in her space-age carrier on the chrome-trimmed booth table.

As Nora'd sat on the opposite side, her arms crossed near the crumpled, grease-stained fast-food wrappers, her dark eyes flashing with mischief as she'd kept him smiling over one Hollywood tale after another.

And there'd been the drive home, that humming black-and-white cruise along inky pavement and snow-blanketed fields, with the radio tuned to a country channel and the conversation tuned to city reminiscing, with Nora's glorious features outlined in passing headlights and her hand settling for an instant on his knee, her laughter nearly erasing the traumas of the day.

How could he have forgotten how much he enjoyed her company?

He shifted to his side with a frown. He hadn't forgotten.

He'd never enjoyed it this much.

He'd spent a miserable day with her under extremely unpleasant and stressful circumstances, and yet here he was, awakened by a colicky baby and cramped in this too-short bed, restless with the anticipation of spending tomorrow with her, too.

Waaah.

He began to slide from beneath the quilts to go to her, to keep her company and offer some moral support—or perhaps take a turn with Ashley in the rocker—but he froze. Too many of his reasons for going out there had to do with that anticipation he was feeling.

And a distinctly unfriendly brand of restlessness.

Suddenly he was all too aware of being alone in the middle of the night with an outrageously attractive woman. A woman who was a cherished, longtime friend.

He turned his back to the door, pressed his head into the pillow and cringed through the cries from the front room. Tomorrow he'd do what he needed to do to keep Fitz and Greenberg happy, and then he'd get the hell out of Dodge.

NORMALLY, IF ASHLEY decided to continue dozing after a predawn snack, Nora would take a cue from her daughter, snuggling into her still-warm bed and luxuriating in the aimless, liquid drift back to sleep. But this morning she was too charged with energy, too aware of the guest in her house.

Much too aware.

She rushed through her shower, belted a thick robe over a T-shirt and sweats and slipped quietly into the dim kitchen. He'd be wanting coffee, she thought as she measured the richly scented grounds and added water to the carafe. And she wanted to make amends for last night's dinner disaster by preparing a decent breakfast.

No, not a disaster, she thought with a smile as she scoured spaghetti sauce from the counter. An extremely unpleasant experience.

Today would be different. Already the morning light was touching the dark window with pewter and clearing the shadows from the mountains' craggy peaks. The stars fading into the dawn promised more crisp, clear weather and a chance for an invigorating walk through crunching snow.

Perhaps there would be chances for several wonderful moments today, moments like those she'd shared with Burke over burgers last night. More relaxed visiting, more laughter. She'd coax him into spending more time with Ashley—he seemed to be warming up to her, in his funny, formal way.

Smiling over the memory of the desperate relief on Burke's face when she'd rescued him from diaper duty, she stacked the rinsed dishes and wiped her hands. They'd all had a rocky start yesterday, but things had ended well.

She breathed in the pitchy tang of the wood she added to the stove and the sulfur-scented flare of the match. A fire would add its special warmth to the cozy space, and the scrambled eggs Jenna had taught her to make would fill their stomachs.

Fresh-squeezed juice, too. She pulled the little juicer from a drawer, gathered the breakfast supplies she'd tossed into the grocery cart yesterday and then turned to see Burke standing in the hallway.

"Good morning," she said with a smile.

"Good morning," he said as though he disagreed.

She halved several oranges and set them aside. "Ashley decided to take an early nap, the sun's on its way and we've got all the ingredients here for a fabulous breakfast. Breakfast I can definitely handle. No unpleasant experiences on the menu this morning," she said with a teasing glance over her shoulder.

He set his briefcase on the table and stared out the window. "Just coffee for me, please."

"You'll change your mind when you see what I'm fixing." She carefully broke the first egg against the edge of a small mixing bowl. "See that? Not a single bit of shell. I love this part—cracking the eggs. Nothing like a little violence to start the day with some excitement."

He glanced without comment at her work, and then poured a mug full of coffee and retreated to his spot at the table.

"This is Jenna's recipe, and it's terrific," she said. "I don't make stuff like this for myself very often, but when Ashley gives me a chance to spend some time in the kitchen, I love to practice."

Another peek over her shoulder told her Burke was in one of his moods, and she smothered a sigh. She wouldn't let anything spoil this day. "I'm going to go ahead and make enough for two. You can skip it if you want, but you'll damage my feelings beyond repair if you don't try at least a tiny taste of my cooking."

"All right. I'll have a taste. I'm afraid I don't have much of an appetite this morning."

She peeled the wrapper from a chunk of ham, and then tensed at the quiet click of his briefcase opening. She'd just lost her appetite, too.

"I think we should discuss the contract," he said.

The egg she cracked against the bowl collapsed in a slimy mess, just like all her plans and hopes for the day. She snatched a fork to pick out the little shards of shell. "What about it?"

"I want to know if you have any additional concerns about the timing. Considering your new responsibilities."

"You mean, considering my daughter." So, he'd chosen to distance himself from her baby. Again.

She turned to face him as she wiped her sticky hands on a dish towel. "She happens to mean a great deal more to me than some wrinkle in a contractual obligation."

"I understand." He shoved his glasses a fraction of an inch higher on his nose. "That's why I'm trying to find the best solution for all involved."

"Why don't you discuss it with Ashley?" She tossed the towel aside. "Ask her when it's most convenient for her mother to be gone on location or promotional tours. Ask her about being handed over to a nanny on the set—if she's allowed to be on the set, that is."

He slid a pad of yellow paper from the case. "Arranging for that kind of child care may complicate things a bit at this stage, but if you wish, I'll make a note of some items we can expect to come up for negotiation in the preliminary—"

"Complications. Negotiations." She began to chop the ham, her fingers shaking with temper. "Go ahead. Earn your keep, Burke. Give it your best shot."

"You're running out of time, Nora." His voice was cool and all business. "The studio is getting impatient about the holdup on the distribution rights. If we don't have the key players and elements in place soon, they may pull the rug out from under us before we've even started. And after the investment we've already made in the script development…"

"You're missing one of your key pressure points here." She slapped a chunk of butter in the frying pan before grabbing the knife to hack through a bunch of green onions. "Aren't you going to remind me how much I owe Fitz? How hard he fought to keep me in the film last summer?"

She dropped the knife and turned to face him. "I know what happened in the hospital the day I almost lost Ashley. I know all about the way he took on the director, and the producer, too."

"He's always wanted what's best for you."

"Yes, he's an amazing, fabulous friend. Loyal and generous to a fault." She narrowed her eyes in a murderous glare. "But he doesn't know what's best for me. Only I know that."

"All right. That's a good place to start." Burke picked up his shiny pen and gave it an annoying click. "Tell me what you want."

"I want you to put that pen away, get that briefcase off my kitchen table, sit down and eat the food I put in front of you."

He frowned and slowly realigned the notepad on the table in a precise parallel to the edge of his briefcase. He placed the pen on top of the notepad in a perfectly centered diagonal.

She fought back the urge to pitch his carefully arranged things out the window.

"What about the role?" She shoved the ham and onion bits into the pan and turned up the heat. "Aren't you forgetting the part about how this role is going to do marvelous, wonderful things for my career? How it's going to help me stretch as an actor? How I'm going to find a new audience and thrill my current fans?"

"I'm not going to discuss the role with you. You may discuss that—and the details of your requested perks—with your agent."

"With my agent?"

"Yes."

"Why won't you discuss those things with *me?*" She yanked open a drawer and grabbed a whisk to beat the eggs. She was looking forward to beating something.

"Because I'd prefer to keep our professional association and our personal relationship separate."

She spun around to stare at him. "Separate?"

"As separate as possible."

"Do you think that's possible?" White-hot sparks of temper burst like fireworks at the edges of her vision.

He nodded in his serious and reasonable way. "I think anything's possible, if two people are willing to try."

How could he stand there, studying her so calmly, and not see how angry she was? She was vibrating with the effort of maintaining a polite expression, struggling to force air past vocal cords primed for a scream. "Oh, I'm trying, all right. I'm trying as hard as I can to be *professional.*"

She was tempted to let him have it, with both barrels. Whip up a storm of a scene, give him a sample of a temperamental rage, something to shake that I'll-make-a-note-of-it cool, that separated-into-neat-little-compartments composure. Something to tilt the balance of their *professional* association and add a new dimension to their *personal* relationship.

A little something to remind him he was dealing with a hell of an actress.

"Nora."

"What?"

"Whatever you put in that pan is burning."

She stared at the smoking ruins of the breakfast she'd begun to prepare with such optimism, and the sight lit a match to the fuse coiled deep inside. The layers of control she'd gathered over herself for all these months sputtered and flared in a white-hot blaze. It had been nearly a year—long months of a fragile pregnancy and weeks of conscientious motherhood—since she'd indulged in the wicked intoxication of a full-blown temper tantrum.

"I'm trying to be *professional*," she said as she grabbed the pan and tossed it into the sink, breaking a few of the dishes stacked below with a satisfying crash, "but I guess I'm a little out of practice."

He lifted one eyebrow in that faintly patronizing arc—gasoline on the fire.

"Besides," she said, "I've never been very good about keeping my *professional* life separate from my *personal* life." She hurled the orange halves and onion stalks toward the sink, missing on purpose, and they bounced off the backsplash and spread in a jumble over the counter. "Considering that *my professional self is the same person as my personal self.*"

She grabbed the mixing bowl and threw it to the floor, where it exploded in bits of crockery and gooey yellow. It felt so good to let go, to let loose, to vent the tiresome frustrations and the nagging fears, to quit playing the role of the polite guest and the grateful recipient of charitable shelter and meals. To play the role of the spoiled brat for a change. No one else could play it as well or with such style.

Too bad her heart didn't seem to be in it this morning. Her anger was already cooling, her battle lust nearly extinguished. But she couldn't quit the stage yet, not until her audience was on his knees, begging for mercy.

Burke leaned his hip against the table in a casual pose and slowly folded his arms across his chest. "I never suggested they weren't."

"No, that's right," she said as she kicked the nearest chair on its side. He flinched a bit at the thud, but he held his ground. "You haven't suggested anything at all. You're too busy *telling* me what I should do."

She whirled and seized the flour canister and sent it skidding across the counter, into the sink. A choking cloud rained white specks over the mess on the floor.

"I won't have it. I won't." She flung one arm wide, knocking a container of stirring utensils into the air. Burke shifted slightly to one side to avoid an airborne spatula and then settled back into his placid pose.

"If you have anything to say to me, to *suggest* to me, you suggest it to *me,* not to my agent," she said as she tossed her hair out of her eyes. "Got that?"

"Yes."

"Well, then?" She took a swaggering step in his direction, avoiding the wreckage as best she could, but a strange self-consciousness swept over her. When she'd made a scene before, Ken had always joined in the shouting, storming about and adding to the excitement, contributing to the overall effect. But Burke was... Burke. Calm. Cool. Dispassionate.

Amused.

Damn. She'd overplayed the scene and underestimated her audience. Her mouth trembled on a giggle, and she clamped down and tried to maintain her fiercest expression.

"Well...what?" he asked.

She moved in close and jutted her chin toward his. "What do you think of that?"

"I think you missed a spot."

He reached for the pepper shaker on the table, unscrewed the lid and dumped the contents over the floury, eggy shards of crockery.

She stared at the mound of black powder, and then at his bland expression, and then she laughed and threw her arms around his neck, loving him, delighted with her patient, clever, wonderful, special, dear friend all over again.

"Oh, you horrible—" she kissed him on the cheek "—awful—" and on the other cheek "—dreadful man." She grabbed him by the hair and pulled his mouth down for a loud, smacking kiss on the lips. "Mmm, I ought to—"

He wrapped his long fingers around her arms and held her in place, trapping her face a few inches from his. "Stop toying with me, Nora."

"I'm not."

He raised that same eyebrow, and she realized, too late, that she'd misjudged the look in his eyes.

"I'm not making a suggestion." He tugged her another fraction of an inch closer, and her breasts brushed against his chest. "I'm *telling* you."

She lowered her hands, shocked and thrilled to see her fingers tremble as she spread them over his crisp white shirt. Beneath the fabric, beneath his warm skin, his muscles were smooth, hard, taut.

She felt them bunch and shift as he tightened his grip on her. As he breathed.

A reckless tension coiled through her again, another short fuse spiraling dangerously close to another powder keg of emotion. Her pulse hammered as she narrowed the charged gap between them to nip at his lower lip in a foolhardy dare.

"Go ahead, then," she whispered. *"Tell me."*

CHAPTER NINE

SHE ALL BUT HEARD his control snap, and then that ferocious focus of his bore down upon her in a glorious assault of mouth and hands and a lean, powerful body pressing hers against the table. With a violent sweep of his arm he hurled everything over the edge—paper, pen, napkins, salt, toys, briefcase—and it fluttered and clattered and crashed to the floor as he sprawled over her, his mouth fused to hers, his lips ravaging, his tongue plunging deep and hot and fast.

She'd never have guessed at the inferno raging inside that cool and controlled exterior. It pumped from him to sear through her, licking like flames along her skin, bubbling through her veins. She strained toward him, seeking more of his heat, craving the flashpoint, answering him with a fiery blast of her own, demanding more, needing more.

"More." She nearly sobbed the word.

His hands fisted in her hair and his teeth scraped along her jaw, and she clawed at his shirt, desperate to get her hands on flesh. One button popped, and another, and she shuddered and groaned with the jolting arousal and the mad, dark pleasure. Skin, at last— fevered satin, coarse hair, ridged muscle and sinew. Raw, rough, exhilarating, male. *Burke.*

A tremor ran through him at her touch, and he kicked aside another chair and shifted higher, yanking at the sash on her robe, cursing at the knot, sinking into another punishing, tormenting kiss, tangling his legs with hers. The table creaked and groaned beneath them, and she struggled for breath, inhaling the scents of citrus and wood smoke, of shower-fresh soap on heated skin.

She arched against him, shuddering as his hand shoved inside her wrap and beneath the next layer to streak up her side and close over her breast, kneading, tormenting, driving her wild—

Making her milk come in.

"Burke," she mumbled against his mouth.

"Mmm?"

"Burke." She shoved at him and twisted to the side, clamping an arm over the stains spreading across her shirt front.

"God." He straightened and stared, and his face went pale. "Did I do that?"

"Yes."

"I'm sorry." He began to wipe his hand against his pants and then froze, flushing a deep crimson.

"Don't be." She pulled the shirt from her chest and frowned at the twin damp spots. "It's perfectly natural."

"It is?"

"I guess so."

She sighed deeply as she tugged her clothing back into place, and then rolled off the table to stagger a step on shaky legs. Heart pounding, system thrumming, she was still riding a giddy high, was still reeling with desire and already missing the feel of his hands on her. "I wouldn't know for sure," she said. "I haven't exactly had a lot of hot-and-heavy necking sessions since Ashley was born."

"I said I was sorry for causing the…well."

He cleared his throat, and then he leveled his solemn gaze at her. "I should probably say I'm sorry for kissing you, too."

The chill that moved through her had as much to do with his careful, guarded words as it did with her soaked shirt front. Damn those stiff and formal manners of his. Why did he have to shut himself away from her, just when he'd given her a glimpse of something vibrant and exciting, something she wanted to explore in more detail? "I wish you'd stop apologizing for every little thing," she said.

His shuttered expression slammed back into place. "You're right. I apologize far too often, for the most ridiculous things."

"Burke, I—"

He reached up to adjust the glasses on his nose, and once he had them straightened, the old Burke was back in place, too.

"I thought I heard Ashley," he said. "You'd best check on her."

BURKE SCOOPED another jumble of flour and sticky pieces of bowl into the dustpan and dumped the lot in the trash container like a penance, berating himself from every possible angle for kissing Nora.

Not just kissing her, to be precise, but coming frighteningly close to ripping that ridiculous outfit from her delicious skin and burying himself deep inside her.

He dreaded facing the consequences of his actions, feared the damage he may have done to their relationship. He was her friend, not some guy on the make. She was his friend, not an object of desire.

Okay, scratch that last bit. Desire was definitely one of the things he was feeling. There it was, simmering hot and thick right below the surface.

Could friends feel this kind of passion for each other and retain the friendship they'd always enjoyed? How could they continue their current relationship with all this…all this insane, volatile lust swirling around them and inside them, waiting to swamp them when they least expected it and suck them down somewhere they had no business going?

Business. God, there was that, too. He was a producer, and she was an actress he wanted to sign for a film project. What a cliché—and one of the worst of Hollywood's tawdry traditions.

What would Fitz think? And Greenberg? Fitz would kill him for laying hands on her, and Greenberg wouldn't let a funeral prevent him from firing the mutilated remains.

And beyond all that, or beneath all that— he couldn't keep the layers of mistakes in order when they continued to pile on top of each other in an untidy heap—there was the fact that he'd made a move on an incredibly vulnerable woman, a recently divorced single mother.

He set the broom back in its corner spot in the pantry and curled his hands into guilty fists. A nursing mother. What kind of a cad would force his attentions on a woman and cause her body to react in such a way, to embarrass her as he had?

He'd told her he wanted to apologize for kissing her, but he wasn't sorry, not at all. He'd wanted to kiss her. He'd realized, in that electrifying instant he'd first covered her mouth with his, that he'd wanted to kiss her for months. For years. Possibly since the moment he'd met her.

What man wouldn't want to kiss Nora Daniels, to shove his hands into that thick mane of raven-black hair and pull that luscious body snug against his? She was every man's fantasy, after all. And he was just a man. A weak and hungry man.

And what kind of a monster would be standing here, in the front room of her house while she nursed her baby, wanting with every randy molecule of his traitorous body to get his filthy, treacherous hands on her again, to pull her close and fill his arms with those pillowy curves, to slip his tongue into her mouth and—

No.

He snatched the phone from the side table and stalked down the short hall to his room. He shut the door behind him, leaned against it and punched the long-distance sequence for Fitz's private cell.

"Burke?"

"Sorry to call you this early, but it's... there's been a—"

"Ellie?"

"No." He dropped to the bed. "God, no—she's fine. Sorry."

"Okay." There was a long pause as Fitz sucked in and let out a deep breath. "Okay, then. What's up?"

"I can't do this anymore." Burke sprang up to pace the tiny room. "I've got to get out of here."

"What happened?"

"You don't want to know."

"Good." Fitz yawned. "Then this is going to be a really short conversation."

"I'm serious, Fitz."

"So what else is new?" The actor gave an impatient sigh. "Buck up and cut the whining. How bad can it be? You've got a roof over your head. And you're getting fed, right? Better than you usually eat, even when I'm doing the cooking. I told you, Jenna's amazing."

"Yes, she's wonderful. They're all wonderful," said Burke. "It's like living in a Norman Rockwell painting of the inside of a freezer."

"So buy some warmer clothes and stay in the frame. Hang in there, Burke. It won't last forever."

"You're not going to let me off the hook here, are you?"

"I need you to do this."

"I told you, I can't. I won't." Burke stopped and pinched the bridge of his nose, bumping his glasses out of place. "Sorry, Fitz, but I won't."

"You've never let me down before."

"I'm aware of that. That's one of the things that makes this so hard." He gripped one of the iron knobs on the bed's foot rail and squeezed. "I quit."

"Come on, Burke, you don't mean that." Fitz swore. "So she's not taking it well, so she's being difficult. Nora's a tricky one, always has been. But she'll come around. She has to, eventually, and she knows it. Try another approach."

"I did." Burke squeezed the bed frame

until his knuckles turned white. "I kissed her."

"You what?"

"I kissed her."

"On the mouth?"

"Yes. And…yes."

"And *what?*"

"Nothing."

"I don't like the sound of that *nothing*. It doesn't sound like *nothing* to me." Fitz paused. "You're not saying anything."

"I don't have anything to say."

"Nothing to say, like, 'I made a mistake,'" said Fitz, "or 'I don't know how it happened,' or 'it'll never happen again'?"

"No." Burke released his grip on the bed. "Nothing like that."

Another ominous pause. *"You're fired."*

"You can't fire me, because I quit."

Fitz launched a stream of curses he must have picked up from Greenberg. "Damn it, Burke. I sent you out there because I trusted you. Because Nora trusts you. Because you're Mr. Cool-Under-Fire, Mr. Ice, Mr.—"

"Just because I prefer to keep my feelings and relationships private doesn't mean I don't have them."

"Don't go getting that snotty Brit attitude

with me," said Fitz. "And what makes you think you're going to keep things private if you get caught making out with Hollywood's next big thing?"

A nasty trickle of ice slithered down Burke's spine, and he did some cursing of his own.

"Okay, okay," said Fitz. "Let's both calm down. Let me think about this for a— *No*. Don't want to go there. *God,*" he said with a groan. "Give me a minute. There's got to be a way to deal with this. To get around this."

"There's no getting around what happened."

"There's got to be a way. Damn it, Burke, I've never fired anyone before."

Burke moved toward the room's curtained window. "I told you, I quit."

"You can't quit." Another soft curse. "And anyway, there's no way to quit a friendship."

His friend sounded miserable, which made Burke miserable, too, more miserable, anyway, than he'd already been feeling, which he hadn't thought was possible.

He pulled a curtain panel to one side and squinted against the glare of the sun sliding over the serrated edge of the mountain range. "I thought we were discussing our working relationship."

"It's one and the same."

"Maybe that's the problem."

"The only problem here is you kissing Nora." Fitz's sigh was deep and unhappy. "Are you going to do it again?"

The longing for her still pulsed through him. Burke wrinkled the curtain in his fist. "If she'll let me."

"Damn."

"You can see why I've got to leave, can't you?" He dropped the curtain back into place, plunging the room back into semidarkness. "I can't use that—the kissing—to get her to sign that contract. That's why I can't do this."

"If you don't get her to sign, Greenberg might move his latest discovery into your bungalow on a permanent basis."

"What?" Burke's gut clenched. "Who?"

"Some kid who's supposed to be a whiz with film budgets." Fitz muttered something unpleasant about Greenberg. "You'd better hurry up and get that signature and get the hell back here."

"I'm not worried about Greenberg. And if the worst happens, I won't starve." He shifted the phone to his other ear. "I've had some offers."

"So I've heard."

Of course he had. Hollywood could show Tucker a thing or two about small-town gossip.

"God, what a mess," said Fitz with another sigh. "Tell me this much—did she kiss you back?"

"Yeah." Burke couldn't stop the grin that spread across his face. "Oh, yeah."

"God help you."

"Thanks. I'll need it."

"Yeah, you will," said Fitz, "'cause you're stuck, but good."

"What?"

"You're going to have to stay right where you are now, at least until I figure something else out."

"*What?*"

"Well, you can't leave now, can you? What will Nora think?"

Burke sank to the bed.

"Think how shaky she must be feeling right now," Fitz continued. "A new mother, on her own, with the scars still fresh from an ugly divorce. Are you telling me you're going to kiss her the way I think you kissed her, and then make a run for the nearest exit—hell, the nearest airport, scrambling to hightail it out of the state?"

Burke swallowed. "I hadn't thought of that."

"No, you were too busy doing 'nothing' to notice what you've gotten yourself into here."

"God." He rubbed his hand across his forehead. "What *have* I gotten myself into?"

"Guess you won't know the answer to that until you figure it out, now, will you?"

He wouldn't run out on Nora when she was so vulnerable, the way Ken had left her when she needed him most. He wouldn't, couldn't do that to her.

"Fitz."

"Yeah?"

He straightened and adjusted his glasses. "I withdraw my resignation."

"I thought you might, under the circumstances. Now, get back to work. You're right about the contract. You can't discuss that with her. But you've still got a budget to come up with."

Burke stood and paced to the dresser, where he aligned the edge of a picture frame with the edge of the dresser's top. "Greenberg is expecting me to produce Nora's signature."

"You leave Greenberg to me."

"No." Burke curled his hand into a fist and

slid it into his pocket. "I told you I'm done with that."

Fitz paused. "Getting a little pushy for someone who nearly got fired a few minutes ago, aren't you?"

Burke set his teeth and waited his friend out.

"Oh, all right," said Fitz with a sigh. "Go ahead and do what you think you have to, get yourself fired for real. But if you hurt Nora— and this is no idle threat, believe me—losing your job will be the least of your worries."

BURKE STEPPED from his room just as Nora exited hers, carrying Ashley. They were both bundled into padded pink jackets, ready for a trip outside.

Lust plowed into him and nearly sent him, begging, to the floor. He locked his knees and paused with the phone dangling from his hand. "I cleaned up the kitchen as best I could."

Nora rolled her eyes as she moved past him. "You didn't have to do that."

"I know."

"And you don't have to mope around, feeling guilty."

"I don't mope. And I'm not feeling guilty." Not since the conversation with Fitz. There was no room for guilt on top of everything else he was feeling right now.

He set the phone back in its stand on the table and slid his hands into his pockets. "Do you think I should? Feel guilty?"

She lifted Ashley's carrier to the table and began to fasten the harness over the baby. "Now, there's an interesting question."

He waited for her answer, but she didn't offer one.

"I'm going to drive into Butte," he said, because he couldn't say it didn't matter where he went, as long as it was somewhere else. "There must be an office-supply store there that's open today."

"I hate to see you waste the time and money." Nora frowned. "I'm sure Ellie would let you use anything in the ranch-house office that you need. Besides, you're only going to be here a short while longer, anyway."

"Are you asking me to leave?"

"My house, or Montana?"

He smiled and relaxed fractionally at the bite in her tone. "Your house."

"It's not really my house, is it?" She sighed and tucked a couple of toys into the giant black diaper bag.

"What did you mean when you said I wouldn't be here much longer?" he asked. "Does that mean you're going to sign the contract?"

She shook her head. "I'm going to think about it, which I'll admit I haven't been doing. But I'm not going to let you rush me into anything. I don't care how good you are at kissing."

She shot him a sultry glance, and his legs nearly buckled again as all the blood in his body rushed to one central location.

"I liked kissing you," he said. "I want to do it again."

"Well, you can't." She picked up the carrier and headed toward the door. "I'm starving. I'm going to go beg for food across the creek at the normal, functional people's house."

"Nora, wait, I—"

She paused with her hand on the knob. "Burke, I don't know how we're going to deal with this—this *thing* that happened between us. But I want to try. I don't want to lose your friendship over something that probably wouldn't have happened if I hadn't gotten a little crazy and out of control."

"You don't have to feel guilty," he said.

"Okay. I don't." Her smile was brilliant. "Boy, that was easy."

She opened the door and stepped outside. "Have fun in Butte. Drive safe. See you later."

The door shut behind her. He couldn't figure out if she'd meant to slam it or not, just as he couldn't figure out what the hell had just happened.

CHAPTER TEN

AN HOUR AFTER Burke had nearly ravished her on the kitchen table, Nora carried Ashley into the ranch house. The scent of baking vanilla and sugar mixed with faint traces of bacon and coffee. "Hello. Is anyone here?"

"In the kitchen," called Jody. "We're making Valentine's Day cookies."

"There's my angel." Jenna rounded the corner, wiped her hands on a dish towel and pulled the baby from the carrier as Nora added her outerwear to the collection of jackets, hats and gloves on the mudroom rack. "It feels like it's been days and days since I've seen you."

"It's only been one," said Nora. Only one day. One long, eventful day and an interesting morning. "But you're right. It feels like it's been a week."

Jenna narrowed her eyes as she hugged the baby. "What happened?"

"No fair talking where I can't hear you," said Jody.

Nora strolled into the kitchen and headed for the coffeepot on the counter. "Any breakfast leftovers?"

"I thought you picked up groceries in town yesterday," said Jenna. "And where's Burke?"

"Probably headed to Butte by now." Nora dropped thick slices of Jenna's homemade bread into the toaster. "He needs some things for work."

"Didn't he check Ellison's?"

"Sam's out of town," said Ellie as she clomped down the service stairs. "And Burke's welcome to use the office here. He knows that."

"He wants to work from his laptop."

Jody shook her head with a worldly sigh. "Sounds like he just needed an excuse to get away."

"Well, I'm glad he came up with one," said Nora, "'cause I was ready to toss him out on his ear if he apologized one more time."

"What's he been doing that he needs to keep apologizing for?" Jenna handed Ashley to Ellie and picked up her rolling pin. "What's going on?"

"Nothing," said Nora. "That's the point. But I'm getting tired of hearing 'I'm sorry' and 'thank you' and 'yes, please' over and over again. The polite act is driving me crazy."

"No one should have to put with that kind of abuse," said Ellie. "Good manners are a perfectly good reason for kicking someone out of your house."

Nora scraped butter over her toast. "You had to be there."

"No, thank you," said Ellie as she wiped Ashley's chin. "I'll take your word for it."

"Maybe he wanted to get away from Ashley," said Jody. "I don't think he likes her."

"I didn't think so, either, at first." Nora leaned against the counter and bit into her skimpy breakfast. "But I think he's coming around. He changed her diaper last night."

"Burke?" Ellie grinned. "I would've liked to have seen that."

"He was kind of cute about it. After he finished apologizing half a dozen times for using her pajamas to wipe up an accident."

Jenna tsked as she cut heart shapes from the flattened dough and lifted them to a cookie sheet. "Why would he do a fool thing like that?"

"He panicked. I left him in charge, and he grabbed the first thing he could put his hands on."

"Do you think that's wise?" Jenna slid the tray into the oven. "Leaving him alone with the baby like that?"

"Anyone who's dealt with Fitz all these years can handle a baby for five minutes." Ellie finger-combed Ashley's curls to one side. "Besides, he's one of the most trustworthy people I've ever met."

"Hmm." Jenna's lips pinched in a tight line. "Did he tell you why he's here?"

Nora picked up her coffee. "There's a contract he wants me to sign."

"Is it for that movie you told me about?" Jody added a few drops of food coloring to a bowl of icing. "You're going to do it, right? It sounds great."

"What movie is this?" Jenna worked the dough for the next batch of cookies.

"A romantic comedy. For Fitz's new company."

"That does sound great." Ellie stood and handed Ashley to Jody. "I was on my way out to stretch my legs a bit," she said with a glance in Nora's direction. "Care to join me?"

"Who's going to help me decorate all these cookies?" asked Jody.

"They'll still be there when we get back."

Nora followed Ellie into the mudroom and bundled back into her jacket, scarf, hat and mittens, and then waited for Ellie to finish fastening her coat around her bulging middle. "Pardon me for stating the obvious, but you're getting huge."

"You should have seen me with Jody. I looked like I was expecting a sumo wrestler."

"Don't tell Fitz his kid is puny, or you'll give him an inferiority complex."

"Kelleran? Never happen."

They stepped out on the back porch, and Nora reached for Ellie's hand to steady her down the steps.

"Where should we head first?" asked Ellie. "The calving barn or the stables?"

"Any place but the barn."

Ellie grinned. "I heard it made quite an impression on Burke."

"Rowdy was the one trying to make the impression. The calving was just a bonus."

"Poor Burke." Ellie led the way along the path past the foreman's cabin. "I asked Fitz what Burke had done to get himself banished, but he wouldn't say."

"It's my fault." Nora wedged her mitten-covered hands into her pockets. "Fitz wants me to sign, and I won't commit."

"Why not? Don't you like the part?"

"No, that's not it. You and Jody are right—it's a great part. A smart career move, too, since I've never done anything like it before."

"Don't you want to work for Fitz?"

"No, that's not it, either."

They trudged on for a few more yards as Nora silently ran through her worn-out list of reasons for avoiding the commitment Fitz wanted her to make. "Anyway," she said at last, "that's why Burke is here."

"Because Fitz is too chicken-livered to pin you down himself."

Nora smiled. "Have I mentioned lately how glad I am you agreed to marry him?"

"Not lately." Ellie stopped and pressed her fists to her lower back. "Now, why don't you talk about the stuff I had to drag you all the way out here to listen to?"

Nora frowned and kicked at a clump of snow. "It's Burke."

"Did he try something?"

"Like what?"

"Like something that wasn't on Fitz's agenda."

Nora sucked in a breath, let it out again. "He kissed me."

"I figured it was going to be something like that."

"You did?"

Ellie waved away her question. "Did you kiss him back?"

"Yes."

Ellie studied her for a long moment. "Hmm."

"What?"

"I was going to ask you if you liked it, but I figured if you *had* liked it, he wouldn't be on his way to Butte and you wouldn't be standing out here, with me." Ellie tilted her head to one side. "But then I figured the opposite might be true."

"He apologized—actually apologized for practically bringing me to a climax with his mouth—"

"Wow."

"No, wait, it's not what you're thinking. We were on the kitchen table, and—"

"Wow."

"No, that's not—"

"You weren't on the kitchen table?"

"Well, yes, but—"

"Go, Burke." Ellie grinned. "Didn't know he had it in him."

"Took me by surprise, too." Nora's eyes

narrowed to slits. "And then my milk came in, and he got all stiff and formal and obnoxious and told me to go check on the baby."

"Poor Burke." Ellie's grin widened. "That must have been a shock."

"What's with all this 'poor Burke' stuff? I was mortified." Nora stepped away and then turned back again. "What am I going to do?"

"What do you want to do?"

"Drag him off to bed."

Ellie shook her head. "He won't go easy."

"I know. And I have no business doing that to a friend. Someone I want to keep as a friend, anyway." Nora shook her head. "That strategy didn't exactly work out too well with Ken."

That was one of the things about the divorce that hurt the most: the fact that she'd lost a friend. She and Ken had had their problems—what couple didn't?—but something had gone terribly wrong. She'd stopped agreeing, and he'd started insisting; she'd stopped listening, and he'd started shouting. She'd stopped being the person he'd wanted her to be, and he'd stopped wanting her at all.

"That was Ken," said. Ellie. "This is Burke."

"Much, much scarier." For too many reasons Nora didn't want to examine at the moment.

She huffed out a breath. "Speaking of scary, what do you think Fitz'll do when he finds out?"

"Kill him. Probably with some torture involved. And then chop the body into little pieces and scatter the bits where they'll never be found."

"That's what I was afraid of." Nora stared at Ellie. "You're not going to tell him, are you?"

"And ruin the fun of watching Burke get so stiff with guilt that he cracks up all over and splinters into a million pieces at Fitz's feet? Nah."

Nora grinned. "You're really scary, you know that?"

"Gotta keep Kelleran in line." Ellie blew on her hands. "Ready to go back inside and confess all to my temporarily stiff and obnoxious former mother-in-law? Except the part about the kitchen table. I wouldn't mention that, if I were you."

"Don't worry."

They turned and headed back toward the tall white house with the steeply pitched gables and touches of gingerbread tacked in the corners. When Nora had first seen it, she'd fancied it looked like something from a storybook, a house that sheltered a fairy-tale family.

She blinked back a sudden, hot film of tears. "I love your mother, Ellie. I wish sometimes she were mine."

"She's just as much yours as she is mine, you know?" Ellie ran a hand down Nora's sleeve. "She just scooped me up and took me in when I was a girl, much the same as she's taken you in these past months."

"And you never left."

"I never had a need to." Ellie paused and stared at the big house. "Where is your mother, Nora?"

"I don't know. She sent a note at Christmas, letting me know she'd be staying with a friend in Monte Carlo for New Year's." Nora glanced at Ellie. "She's never once asked about Ashley. When I told her I was pregnant, she was horrified I was going to make her a grandmother."

"I'd say I'm sorry, but I don't want to get kicked."

Nora smiled and sniffed. "I don't want to hurt Jenna."

"You won't, not as much as you think you might."

Ellie rubbed a mittened hand over her protruding belly. "Fitz has been trying like crazy to pry her loose from this place for a visit to California. Maybe if you were there to show her a good time, she'd take him up on one of his invitations."

They crossed the wide graveled drive. "I don't see you flying out there very often," said Nora.

"Yeah, I know," said Ellie with a shrug. "It's not like I don't get plenty of invitations. But I want to be here for Jody. Fitz understands."

"I want to be there for Ashley, too." Nora sucked in a deep, wavery breath. "I want to be a good mother. I didn't know how, and I'm still terrified of making a mistake. I thought I could soak up everything I needed to know from you and Jenna. That's one of the reasons I haven't left."

She ran her cold, fuzzy, mittened hand under her nose. "I've been using you all. I've abused Fitz's hospitality and taken advantage of your kindness, and I've given nothing back. To any of you."

"Oh, I wouldn't say it's been nothing," said Ellie as they neared the back porch steps. "You've given us plenty of laughs, when we knew you weren't looking."

Nora gave her shoulder a friendly shove.

"And you're the bait that brought Burke here." Ellie's grin widened. "Looks like he's going to give us plenty more."

BURKE SAT HUNCHED OVER his laptop keyboard in the molded plastic booth of a fast-food restaurant in Butte, doing his best to ignore the cake-smearing, soda-spitting, balloon-waving, shoulder-shoving, name-calling, ear-piercing pandemonium of a birthday party at the next table. The clerk at the office-supply store had assured him this place was the only spot in the entire city that offered a public wireless connection.

He scrolled through his e-mail in-box, checking for important messages, responding to the most urgent, downloading files for further use. Hoping, as he lowered the screen to protect it from an incoming French fry, that he could take care of his business and make his escape with his sanity intact.

He tried not to think about how he might be spending this Sunday afternoon at home. Relaxing with Fitz on his deck, watching the waves roll in and the bikini-clad neighbors stroll by. Wandering through an art gallery, anticipating an at-home dinner of take-out sushi and an evening of film classics on his wide-screen television. Sprawling in his bed with the paper and deli pastries and the delectable Hannah.

No—*Heather*. The serene, noninfant-toting wardrobe assistant.

The birthday celebration ended with no fatalities, and relative silence descended on the garishly colored dining area. One small family group remained, tucked into a corner across the room—a harried mother with two young boys and an infant in a carrier. The baby kicked its feet and screamed.

The soundtrack of his life these days. A life on ice.   Literally.

He switched to research mode, reorganizing, bracing himself for the worst. Internet providers. Weather forecasts. Colic. Infant development. Nursing mothers. He made a few notes, jotted down addresses and driving directions. He wanted to run a few errands before it was time to head back and report to Granite Ridge for another family dinner. Another meal consisting of constant motion, competing conversations and a screaming infant.

At least there would be no balloons at Jenna's table.

NORA SAT IN THE ROCKER with a howling, arching, red-faced Ashley, dreading the moment she'd have to buckle her into her car seat for the trip to the ranch house.

At times like this, when the heart-wringing cries seemed to vibrate through her body and set off sympathetic stomach pains of their own, Nora doubted everything about herself. About her competence as a single parent, about the viability of her career, about her prospects of ever finding another man to love. A man who'd love her in return, who'd love Ashley, who'd understand the stresses of her career, who'd tolerate the occasional upheavals and provide the necessary support.

A man who'd be there, no matter what. A man who'd stay, no matter what.

The yearning was a terrible pressure in her chest. She burrowed her face into Ashley's overheated neck, fought the threatening tears and rocked harder.

She could do this. She could rebuild her own life, her own way. She could be a competent woman with a successful career, a loving and dependable mother. All she had to do was channel her energy and transform those vague, misty thoughts about her future into a series of clear images. And then work toward those goals, one at a time.

Heavy footsteps on the porch were followed by a four-beat knock on the door. Burke.

"It's open," she called.

He squeezed through the doorway, carrying his briefcase, several shopping bags and a gigantic bunch of soft blue irises. He may not have been the man of her daydream, but he was someone who'd always understood and supported her, no matter what.

A friend.

"For me?" asked Nora.

He shook his head and set the flowers on the table. "For Jenna."

He pulled a plastic sphere resembling a hollow honeycomb from one of the bags. "This isn't for you, either."

"Look, Ashley." Nora peeled her daughter from her shoulder and shifted her to face Burke. "Uncle Burke brought you a present."

He held the ball within the baby's reach. She hiccupped and made a slow, uncoordinated grab for it. Her clumsy fingers poked through the wide openings, and her natural clutching motion allowed her to capture the ball and bring it to her mouth.

"She likes it." Nora gave Burke a grateful smile. "She stopped crying."

"For now, anyway." He reached into another bag and produced four music disks. "These are for you."

Sonatas and concertos, a symphony and a collection of jazz classics. She could already hear the lush, rhythmic notes pouring through the air and brushing over her skin.

"I noticed there's a player on the television stand," he said, "but I don't see any CDs in the house."

Ashley dropped the ball, and he picked it up and held it, patiently, waiting for her to grab it again. "I miss your music, Nora."

"So do I." The pressure in her chest tightened, and she struggled to force the words past the lump in her throat. "Thank you. For everything."

"Here." He lifted Ashley and her new toy from Nora's lap. "I'll hold her for a bit. What time do we have to leave for dinner?"

"In about an hour."

She stood and peeled the wrapper from one of the cases and slid the CD into the player. The opening bars of Moszkowski's concerto rumbled through the room. "You didn't have to buy all these things. But I'm glad you did."

"So am I."

He tipped up her chin with a knuckle. "I'm going to kiss you now, just to prove I can do it without losing my mind. And because I still want to."

She closed her fingers over his wrist. "I still want to kiss you, too."

Their lips met for a brief, bittersweet moment as the music swelled and Ashley writhed and complained. When she opened her eyes, Nora found his locked on hers in a solemn, intense gaze.

"Well," he said with a frown, "there's a start, anyway."

TWO DAYS AGO Burke had sat in this same chair at the Harrison family table. It felt like two weeks ago.

The conversation could warp time on its own.

To his left, Ellie and Will discussed whether to take on temporary help to get them through this shorthanded spell in the calving season. To his right, Jody and Jenna chatted about how to pack and transport decorated cookies to a party. Directly across the table, Maggie tried to soothe a howling Ashley while Wayne forked a second helping of turkey onto his plate.

Nora sat in the seat next to Maggie, right where Burke couldn't ignore her. Tonight she wore a drool-inducing red sweater that clung to and draped over and outlined every soft, curvy inch. She'd left her hair unrestrained, and it cascaded in tousled waves down her back and caressed her shoulders with every move. Tiny drop earrings winked and teased at him as they danced against that tender spot along her jaw—the spot he knew made her whimper when he nipped it. The scent of her cologne added a subtle layer of allure to the steam she was pumping in his direction.

"Earth to Burke."

"Sorry?"

Jody rolled her eyes and handed him a bowl of mashed potatoes. "Pass this to Will, please."

He caught another cool glance from Jenna as he took the bowl from Jody. An unfortunate addition to the evening's ambience, but not enough to keep him from finishing his meal. He'd begun to worry he'd slowly starve during this trip.

"By the way," said Maggie, "Wayne and I found out the sex of the baby."

The conversation around the table sputtered and died.

"It's a boy."

"Congratulations." Will reached across the table to shake Wayne's hand.

"A boy!" Jody let out a whoop. "Have you decided on a name yet?"

Maggie paused and glanced at her husband with a watery smile, and he settled an arm around her shoulders and gave her a squeeze. "We're going to call him Tom," said Wayne. "If that's okay."

"Oh." Jenna snatched her napkin to her mouth. "Oh, my."

Beside him, Ellie bowed her head, and Will swung an arm around her shoulders to hug her close. Jody set her fork slowly and carefully on the edge of her plate and began to sniff.

Within a few seconds, every female in the room was crying as loudly as the baby.

Burke shoved his plate away. Even a starving man couldn't eat under these circumstances.

"I think that's a wonderful idea." Will lifted his wineglass in an awkward toast as Ellie clung to his neck.

Wayne gently pulled Ashley from Maggie's

arms so she could collapse within Nora's teary hug. He settled the baby on his shoulder and stood to fill Will's glass, and then offered the same to Burke.

"I take it the name has some special significance," said Burke.

"He was Maggie's brother," said Wayne. "Ellie's first husband, Jody's father."

"Tom Hammond," said Will. "Has a nice ring to it. Good and solid."

"Maggie and I think so."

The sobs increased in volume.

Burke stared into his glass. He'd thought the freezing temperatures, the baby vomit, the vile stuff in the diaper, the experience in the calving barn and every awful moment in Nora's kitchen had been the worst that could possibly happen to him in Montana.

But he'd been wrong. He'd forgotten about the gestating, lactating, menstruating hormonal tendencies toward maudlin excess. "I'd like to drink to your news," he said, "but I have to admit, the general reception makes the idea a bit uncomfortable."

"Don't let the slobbery stuff bother you." Wayne's lips turned up in one of his shy smiles. "Those are happy tears."

"But—he died."

Will nodded. "And those are the sad tears."

"How can you tell the difference?"

"Does it matter?" Wayne emptied the last of the wine into Will's glass. "That's what this is for."

CHAPTER ELEVEN

NORA MADE ANOTHER CIRCUIT of the cabin's front room, gently jouncing Ashley to sleep with her middle-of-the-night mother's dance step. Step-swing, step-swing. Rock-rock-rock. Her throat was getting a little sore from humming the same tune over and over—something from a television commercial, she realized—and her lower back was beginning to protest. But Ashley's eyelids were beginning to stick a bit whenever they drifted shut, so Nora kept up the pace and the tune. Step-swing, step-swing. *It's your highway, it's your life. Take the wheel and live it.*

"What do you think, princess?" Nora smiled at her daughter as she lost the battle against the drowsiness. "Should we buy that funny-looking car? It gets great mileage."

She danced her way down the hall, to her room, and carefully slid Ashley into her crib. When the baby's eyes fluttered open, Nora stroked a finger from her forehead to the tip of her nose, coaxing her, willing her back to sleep. "It's your highway, it's your life. It's your life."

It's your life. Nora climbed into bed and stared at the shadows fanning from the little night-light on Ashley's dressing table across the ceiling beams. Her life, and Ashley's.

They were a unit. Burke's arrival here and his intrusion into her life had helped her see that. The scene around the Harrison family's dinner table last night had driven the lesson home.

She'd shed tears of happiness for her friend Maggie, Tom's sister, and tears of sympathy for her friend Ellie, Tom's widow, but she'd never known Tom Harrison. No matter how much she may have wished she and her daughter could be a part of that larger unit, part of the Harrison family, she wasn't someone's wife or sister, a mother or a daughter. She was an outsider, like Burke. Like Ashley.

She closed her eyes and pictured herself pacing with Ashley through the grand gathering room of her home in the Hollywood Hills. Step-swing, step-swing, around the plush and pillowed seating area, and the fleamarket finds of the side grouping, through the book-filled alcove and the niche that held the grand piano. Rock-rock-rock, up the graceful sweep of the stone staircase, along the wide hall and through the double doors of the master suite. The city's gridlike constellation would spread below the arched windows, and reflected moonglow would bounce from the surface of the pool to ripple across the vaulted ceiling.

So far to travel, from one spot in the house to another. Shuffling dance steps across floors of marble and teak, the distant swoosh of traffic a counterpoint to her late-night lullaby. So far to travel, from the safe embrace of a cozy cabin in the shadows of the mountains to the echoing, elegant spaces of the house in the hills above the city.

Far to go, but time to move on. Burke's purpose and presence here had proved that, too. He'd brought the ghost of her Hollywood life to her door. And his kiss had awakened in her sensations she'd forgotten.

Shifting to her side, she let herself sink into a softly whirling blend of memories and dreams. She moved again through her Hollywood house, down the photo-lined hall to the kitchen. There was Burke, hunched over the electric-blue glow of his laptop screen at her kitchen table, his white shirtsleeves rolled over sinewy forearms, his black hair fallen across his forehead to brush the rims of his glasses, his forehead creased in concentration. She'd offer him coffee; he'd decline. He'd tap a few keys, close his laptop with a tiny click, place his notepad and pencil on the lid, lined up just so. And then he'd stand and tug her close, wrap her in those strong arms and sway with her in a lovers' dance.

Step-swing, step-swing. Fingertips stroking, lips sampling, breath mingling on a silent hum of anticipation. Yearning toward each other, wanting each other. Taking each other.

It's your highway, it's your life. Take the wheel and live it. The yearning pressed in on her again, stronger and focused. She could satisfy this craving for contact, for comfort. All she had to do was slip out of bed and tiptoe down the hall. All she had to do was seduce Burke.

Seduce her friend.

She rolled to her side and stared at the slats of Ashley's crib and listened to the quiet *tsk, tsk* of the baby's dream sucking. Nora closed a hand over her breast and wondered if Burke

would be able to find the woman beneath the
mother. Would she be able to find herself in
his caress? Or would she remain some kind
of shadowy half person, one half of her tiny
family unit of two?

Tsk, tsk, tsk.

Nora's eyes drifted shut once, twice, and
stuck.

BURKE CHEWED his jam-covered toast on
Monday morning and glanced across the
kitchen table, where Ashley slumped in her
carrier. She whined and arched her back in a
warning signal that told him she was running
out of patience with the babysitting arrangement ahead of schedule. And the snatches of
Nora's off-key shower song rising above the
faint thrum of the water in the pipes told him
she wouldn't be coming out of the bathroom
anytime soon.

He stared at the baby and gave himself a
silent pep talk. He'd watched others undo the
harness and pluck her from her fancy plastic
throne—how hard could it be? He'd get a
firm grasp beneath her arms, balance her to
prevent any damage to that wobbly neck
while being careful not to crush her rib cage,
and then he'd lift her into his lap before she

had time to protest the deal. If he managed to get her out of that contraption and distract her with some conversation, he might prevent the start of a tantrum.

Anything would be better than listening to the baby scream for the next several minutes while his blood pressure soared toward seizure levels.

Anything but another diaper change, perhaps. Or having his nails pried slowly from his fingers, one by one.

Another high-pitched squeal of annoyance had him bolting out of his seat. "Don't cry," he begged as he wrestled with the first catch. "Whatever you do, don't cry. And don't spit up. Or squirt goo out the side of your diaper. None of that unpleasant business, do you understand?"

The second catch proved more difficult than the first, and he cursed and popped a bloodied finger into his mouth to suck on it. "Damn," he muttered. Ashley stared at him with a startled expression. "I mean, *darn*."

A few moments later he'd managed to unhitch the last barrier, and now he faced the delicate battle of working her arms through the shoulder straps without dislocating her shoulders. The squirming baby twisted and stiffened, fighting his efforts.

A bead of sweat trickled down his back. All right, this wasn't as easy as it looked. But it wasn't impossible. Surely calm logic and persistence would solve the problem.

He gently pulled one rubbery little arm free, only to have the baby lurch to her side, her legs dangling over the edge. *"Bloody hell."*

He scooped her awkwardly into his lap and shifted her to her back, remembering to cradle her head. As he leaned forward to adjust her in a more comfortable position, she flung an arm toward his face and accidentally slipped a couple of tiny fingers into his mouth.

They both froze and stared at each other. "I suppose it's too late to ask where those fingers have been," he said with her hand bouncing against his lips.

Her mouth opened wide in one of her gummy smiles, and she answered him with an unmistakable baby laugh.

Burke's ribs seemed to expand and wrap around his heart several times before squeezing it tight. "Do it again," he said, gently pressing her fingertips. "Come on, you annoying little pest, you owe me. Do it again."

Another smile—a wrinkly eyed, full-bodied-spasm of a smile—but no laugh.

He blew on her knuckles, and he made an embarrassing vibrating sound against her palm, and Ashley watched him and smiled, obviously enjoying his ridiculous antics, but she continued to hold out on him.

He hadn't realized that particular female trait was present at birth.

As a last resort, he grabbed her hand and tickled the tip of his tongue over her fingertips—and she rewarded him with another belly laugh.

Amazing. There had never been anything in his life up to this moment that had given him such a rush, such intense pleasure, such spectacular joy as the sheer delight of that fleeting hiccup. Nothing. Not the most satisfying accomplishment, not the most stunning orgasm.

He lifted her close to nuzzle her nose with the tip of his, and her tiny black lashes flickered as her eyes went out of focus and drifted shut.

"God, you're precious," he whispered.

"What are you doing?" Nora stood in the hallway in one of her bulky robes, a towel wrapped around her head and her hand on her hip.

"She laughed at me."

"She did?" She rushed into the room and leaned over his shoulder, staring at her daughter. "Make her do it again."

"I'm not sure I can." He didn't want Nora to know he'd had her daughter's hand in his mouth. Maybe she wouldn't approve of the potential for germs or the intimacy of the contact, or the idea that he'd felt free to experiment with the baby while she was out of the room.

"She's only done it for me a couple of times," said Nora, "and Jenna's only been able to get her to do it once. The first time she did it, I wasn't sure what had happened."

"I'm sure."

Nora wrapped her arms around his neck in a sloppy hug. "It's *amazing,* isn't it?"

He stared at Ashley's tiny fingers, treasuring the memory of the feel of them against his lips, and he knew he'd never forget those moments they'd shared.

He lifted a hand to one of Nora's and gave it a squeeze. "Yes. It is."

JENNA PRESSED A BUTTON on the television's remote control the next morning as Burke worked in the ranch-house office and Nora paced across the second parlor, gently jouncing Ashley in her arms while the baby whined and kicked.

A show about caulking bathroom tile, another about training a dog to heel, one about applying makeup, something about a rock singer fighting a drug addiction… dozens of choices with the new satellite dish Fitz had installed, and still nothing to catch her interest. Just more time wasted looking for things.

Not that she should be sitting here looking for distractions, anyway. She had plenty of distractions in her house as it was.

"Thanks again for letting Burke check his e-mail," said Nora as she tried to get Ashley to take her pacifier. "He tried to figure out a way to get something rigged up at the cabin, but there's really no point, since he probably won't be here for too much longer, anyway."

Jenna chose to ignore the implication that Nora might not be here too much longer, either. "He'd be more than welcome to his own private space right here in this house for all his business, if he wanted."

"He knows that." Nora shifted Ashley to her shoulder and checked her watch. "I can tell he's uncomfortable being such a bother.

This has got to be hard on him—he's usually the one seeing to everyone else's needs."

Jenna shifted on the sofa and told herself to remember that fact—and to remember that she'd always liked the man, too. He'd helped make Jody's twelfth birthday extra special last summer, handling the details of the gift Fitz had chosen. He'd been a steady and loyal friend to the actor through his troubled courtship and an eloquent best man at his wedding. At the reception, filled with goodwill and Fitz's champagne, Jenna had shared with him her hope he'd soon find some woman of his own to love, someone who'd appreciate all his fine qualities.

Danged if she wasn't having trouble making herself remember those fine qualities right now, with that same man making himself at home in the ranch office.

And though she knew he hadn't chosen this trip and hadn't wanted to make it, she couldn't seem to put a stop to her simmering resentment for the reasons he was here. Or to letting some of that resentment bubble over and spread to the man himself. Made it hard to be a good hostess when she wanted her company gone. Especially when the only way she thought she might deal with the situation was to get him out of Nora's house and under her own roof where she could keep an eye on him.

"There's space for a desk in the extra bedroom at the end of the hall," she said. "Will could set up whatever he needed in no time."

Nora stared out the window at the roof of the tiny foreman's cabin visible behind a row of willows. "Or he could replace the water heater."

"That, too." Jenna clicked the remote one more time and found a channel featuring a cooking demonstration. "I'll talk to him about it when he comes in for lunch."

"The thing is," said Nora, "I'm enjoying Burke's company."

"And I'm sure he's enjoying yours." Wouldn't any man enjoy the company of a lively, lonely young woman?

Ashley writhed and fussed, and then emitted a familiar putt-putt sound.

"Well, no wonder she's been carrying on so," said Jenna. "She'll quiet right down now. Want me to change her diaper for you so you can put your feet up for a while?"

"No, thanks." Nora nuzzled her daughter's pink, round cheek. "It's nearly time to feed her, anyway."

Jenna gave the remote one last chance.

She'd rather keep her fingers busy with needlework than push these little buttons. A war movie...a car chase...something in another language...a pretty young woman pulling a baking sheet from an oven. Jenna waited to see what she'd made.

Nora spread the portable changing mat on the sofa beside Jenna. "What is she making?"

"Puff pastry."

"Looks complicated."

"But well worth the fuss." Jenna combed her fingers through Ashley's hair while Nora changed the diaper, making the fluffy curls swirl across her forehead. "I can show you how, if you'd like."

"Maybe someday. Someday in the distant future." Nora shook her head. "I had enough trouble with the spaghetti the other night."

"Why don't you and Burke stay here for the rest of the day and have dinner with us? We could have a nice, long visit while he works, and I've got plenty of food."

"Thanks for the invitation, but there are some things we need to discuss." Ashley whined and arched her back, and Nora lifted her and pulled two cloth diapers from the oversized tote. "The sooner we get things decided, the sooner he can leave."

Jenna tensed. "Are you going with him?"

"That's one of the things we need to decide."

"You know you're welcome to stay as long as you want."

"I do know, and I love you for offering. Believe me, I'm tempted to stay as long as I can."

Jenna picked up the needlework she'd set aside when Nora and Burke arrived. She needed something to do with her hands, something to help quiet the nerves skittering beneath her skin. "Have you given any thought to making a new life for yourself out here?"

"I've treated myself to a daydream or two." Nora stared out the window. "But I have no idea what I'd do to support myself. And Ashley."

"If you met some nice man and got married, you wouldn't have to do much more than what you do now."

"I think most men would want a wife who didn't get knots in her stomach at the thought of putting together a packaged spaghetti dinner." Ashley squawked and rubbed her face against Nora's chest, and she smoothed her hand over the baby's head. "If I couldn't have a career of my own, I'd want to be the puff pastry kind of wife, and I'm not sure I could pull that off."

"Cooking can be learned." Jenna stuck her thumb with the needle and sighed over her clumsiness. "Being a loving wife and a good mother, being the kind of woman who wants to make a comfortable home—those aren't things that come with lessons."

When she stabbed her thumb a second time, she dropped the needlework in her lap. "Those things mean more to a man than what's on his plate come suppertime. And those are the things you have to offer, Nora. Don't you ever sell yourself short."

"I did, once." Nora held Ashley tightly against her as she leaned down to kiss Jenna's cheek. "I won't do it again, I promise."

Burke entered the room and paused in the corner, staring at the baby. "I thought I heard her mad voice."

"She's hungry." Nora smiled and headed for the entry. "Time to go feed my girl."

Her mad voice. Jenna studied the way Burke's gaze followed Nora as she left the room. There was some heat there, but a great deal of affection, too.

The sudden silence seemed awkward. "I

hear you got a smile this morning," Jenna said to fill it.

The way that sober face lit up went a long way toward softening Jenna's heart toward the man.

"Would you like to stay and have some lunch in about an hour?" she asked. "Turkey soup?"

"The turkey from last night's dinner?" He gave her one of his rare smiles. All too rare, thank goodness. The change in his appearance was a bit unnerving.

The man could be devastatingly attractive, if he ever decided to put a little effort into it.

"And fresh cracked-wheat bread," she said, "if you can wait for it to cool after I take it out of the oven."

He lifted his glasses and resettled them on his nose in exactly the same spot. "I don't suppose there's any chance you'd consider relocating to Los Angeles?"

"About the same chance as you deciding to move out here on a permanent basis."

"I could say something about hell freezing over," he said in that oddly formal manner of his, "but now that I've spent some time here, that expression doesn't seem to convey quite the same degree of improbability that it used to."

She smiled and picked up her needlework again as he headed back to the office. Her hands and her heart seemed a little steadier now.

CHAPTER TWELVE

BURKE CLICKED through to another page on the breast-feeding information site he'd found on the Internet, and then froze when he realized the implications of the article he'd selected. Nursing women and sex.

Sex with a nursing woman. With Nora.

A love affair with actress Nora Daniels. Ashley's mother.

It was impossible to unlink the two of them any longer. And he had no business—literally—getting involved with Nora, and certainly not with her child. He twitched the cursor over the disconnect icon…and then shifted it back toward the scroll button, halfway, the cursor hovering accusingly over the text of the article. He read the first line. And the second.

He read to the end of the piece.

The dry scientific discussion on the screen seemed to waver beneath an image of Nora's face and figure, her voice and manner. The biological terms, the physical realities, the emotional ramifications—it threatened to bury desire under so many layers of obstacles and difficulties and risks that he wondered why he was still considering it.

Because beneath those layers, beneath the faint scent of spit-up, and the sleep deprivation, and the noise and confusion and the constant press of responsibility, the desire—the *yearning* for the woman at the center of it all—simply refused to disappear. No amount of self-lecturing or reasoning or research could banish that craving.

He closed the lid on the laptop, shoved out of the ancient wooden desk chair and moved to the tall window with its view of the mountains. Now they were wreathed in ghostly tatters and shadowed in indigo, where a few hours ago they'd been touched with streaks of icy silver and flecks of sunlight's gold. A constantly fascinating, constantly changing tableau of never-changing rock. The view, the image, the perspective and light might change, but the substance, the essence of the range stayed the same.

Certain core things had to stay the same, or the world would fly into chaos. It was a comforting thought, anyway.

He wanted Nora. Whether that desire would turn out to be a part of the surface or the substance of their relationship, he couldn't yet define. Yes, there would be difficulties the first time he took her to bed. He understood what he faced, and why, in dry biological and psychological terms. What he felt for her, what he wanted to share with her—could he sustain that communication through the strain?

Things would have been so much simpler if he'd made his move before she'd met Ken and rushed into marriage. Before she'd had Ashley. If he were to wait another few months, things would be simpler still. There were easier ways of starting a sexual relationship than choosing to do it with a newly divorced nursing woman.

It wasn't his choice alone. Should he ask her? Discuss it with her in those dry, biological and psychological terms? Should he test her reaction with a seduction—and then call a halt to the heated proceedings for a discussion of the next step? Neither of them had handled things well after the episode in the kitchen—would the memories of the aftermath hover like ghosts to cast shadows over the next interlude of kisses and caresses?

Was analyzing affection likely to cool it before he had a chance to express it?

He closed his eyes and rubbed a hand over his heart while the text of the Web site scrolled through his mind and the heat of the memories of Nora on the kitchen table simmered in his blood. Down deep, beneath the chaos of his unanswered questions, he still wanted her.

NORA STEERED HER CART around one of the bins in the produce section of North Town Market, hunting for the few items on Jenna's list. She could have stayed to sit and chat with Jenna after the turkey soup luncheon, but she'd been too restless to face another afternoon tucked away in the house. Too twitchy to sit and knit knowing Burke was in a room a few feet away, plowing though his business—and possibly plotting and planning hers. She'd jumped at the chance to leave Ashley in Jenna's care and come into town on her own.

She had an hour, maybe a little more, before she'd be on Mom duty again. If she were back at the cabin, she'd take the hour to stretch out in her soft bed and indulge in a nap, or to prop up her feet and knit or curl up and read some more of that juicy romance novel with the charming hero. In an hour she could do the dishes and swipe at some dust, start a load of laundry and clear the clutter in the front room.

In an hour she could flip through Burke's script again.

She paused to say hey to a fellow customer and then guided her cart into another aisle. She had to make a decision about that script, and soon. And if not that script, then one of the others stacked in her bureau drawer. She couldn't go on like this, floating in a limbo of diaper changes and household chores.

She could do it today. Or tomorrow. Or by the end of the week. Give herself a deadline and stick to it. Decide on the script, and then decide how to handle everything else—the move, the house, the nanny.

The nanny. Her throat closed up with a familiar ache, and she squeezed her eyes shut. A deadline for handing Ashley over to the hired help while she drove off to spend impossibly long hours on the set. While she traveled on location or crisscrossed the country for premieres and promotional tours.

She'd always known she'd face long and difficult separations from her child, but she couldn't possibly have understood—not until Ashley was born—exactly what that meant. No one could have described this wrenching pain at the thought of saying goodbye to her precious girl. No one could have explained this paralyzing fear of leaving her baby with some who didn't love Ashley nearly as much as she did.

Ashley's father might have provided the necessary love and care, but the divorce had ended those hopes. Ken hadn't once taken advantage of his generous visitation rights. The travel conditions to Montana were miserable, he'd explained, and the restaurant was busier than ever during the holiday season. Eventually he'd stopped bothering with excuses, and Nora had stopped phoning with reports on his daughter's progress.

No, the love and care of a father wasn't likely now. Nora needed to get used to leaving Ashley with others, and learn to do more on her own. She squared her shoulders and pushed her cart to the end of the aisle.

As she rounded the aisle corner, one of the cart's wheels hooked through the wiry legs of a chips display, and she leaned to the side to untangle it. When she straightened, she came face-to-face with The Ghost of Hollywood Past.

A bare-midriff, bad-dye-job, questionable-fashion-sense version of the past, anyway, captured on the cover of everyone's favorite tabloid. An actress who'd snagged a role out from under Nora's nose a couple of years ago. And what was this? An arrow pointing to a slice of exposed skin above a saggy waistband and a caption asking if there was a baby on the way.

Not if there were more roles out there to steal from better talent, there wasn't.

She shoved the cart past the jams and jellies and turned the corner into condiments land, telling herself she should feel sorry for the poor woman. Imagine the mortification. Work up an Amazon River of sweat with a trainer for hours each week, stress over every morsel doled out calorie-by-calorie into a starving body, and then your tiny tummy bulges in front of a lucky paparazzo and there you are, stocked in magazine racks for the masses in the markets to cluck their disapproving tongues at your pudgy middle.

She tossed a small container of mustard into the basket and paused to press a hand to her midsection. Was there a bump? Did she still look pregnant?

Had she lost all the weight she'd put on while she was pregnant? And even if she had, did it look like she had?

Maybe her incredible metabolism—her most closely guarded beauty secret—had gone haywire during the pregnancy, and she'd have to start dieting.

Dieting could be a problem. She'd have to develop self-control before she started. Which meant they'd be lifting her with a crane before she got a handle on her impulses.

Now there was an image for the tabloids.

She pulled a package of frozen bagels from the refrigerator case with a prick of homesickness for the fresh, chewy pastries she used to buy at the neighborhood deli. Bagels and lox, sprinkled with capers—her weekend favorite. She made a mental note to look for lox in the meat department.

Right next to the venison.

Where was she? It had been so long since she'd indulged in a session of self-obsessing she'd forgotten how to sink into her problems and wallow for a while. Oh, yeah—dieting. The body image thing. She'd been too busy lately to give hers a thorough examination in the mirror. Mostly because she didn't care what her muscle tone looked like. To be honest, she'd never paid all that much attention.

Not even when there'd been a man in her life who was busy paying the kind of attention she hadn't.

And why did it matter now? The only person who cared what kind of shape she was in was Ashley.

She added a can of sliced peaches to her small pile of groceries, and then a can of pears. Burke could take his pick. Not the most exciting fare, but healthy.

Health. That's what mattered the most, she told herself as she rounded the aisle and came into contact with the newsstand again. But, oh, just look at that gorgeous cover model. And that gown—bet it was a Balenciaga.

Wonder if Nicolas Ghesquiere ever designed anything for nursing mothers?

Even if he did, she couldn't afford it right now. And she didn't have a reason to wear a designer gown right now, either.

If she did, the captions would probably be eye-catching: Nora Daniels, looking haggard and pregnant again, all dressed up with no place to go. A big red arrow would point to the tummy bump, and another, smaller pointer would draw attention to the circles under her eyes. And to the sagging muscle tone. The nonexistent pedicure.

The nonexistent life.

God, what was she doing to herself, and over a gossip magazine?

She'd been lucky—the photos and captions and pages devoted to her in the past had been so complimentary. According to the press, she was talented, beautiful, stylish, clever. She had a wonderful husband and a beautiful home. A star on the rise, a woman to envy.

Now what would they say about her? Divorced and drab. A single mother without a man on her horizon, an out-of-work actress with mortgage worries. A star on the ropes, a woman to pity.

This was another reason she was in no hurry to go back. If a magazine cover in a grocery store could bring on these stomach-churning self-doubts, what would the face-to-face, larger-than-life business itself do to her?

She was glad she'd escaped, glad to be where she was, living among real people, people who didn't think about buying Balenciaga or examining each other's bumps and lumps. No, she didn't want to go back, wouldn't take a ticket to body-image hell. Why would anyone want to move through the muck with paparazzi and tabloid reporters?

Not that she wouldn't be good at it, she thought as she tossed her hair over her shoulder and grabbed a bag of chips from the end of the aisle. She could dish the dirt with the dirtiest dishers, if she wanted to. Heck, she'd probably be a lot better at it, too.

Maybe she should ask her agent to put out some feelers for a job with an entertainment channel. Jody could be her sidekick. They'd make a great team, give the other red carpet crews a run for their money.

Jody was a great one for questions. She'd asked some doozies during those weekend afternoons she'd smuggled her tabloids into the cabin for a private gossip fest. *How did you get your start? What makes you want this bad enough to put up with the crazy stuff? What would you be doing if you weren't acting?* And Nora could ask the other important questions: *Where did you get those shoes? Do you think big shoulders will ever make a comeback?*

Okay, so she missed it. A little. She missed the pink-icing architecture and the palm trees, the competitive partying and the glitter in the shop windows.

And she had friends there. Good friends, like Muzzy Campbell and the Fleischners. And Fitz and Burke.

Technically, Burke shouldn't be on that list, because he was here, instead of back in California, where he belonged.

She frowned at the meat in the glass display case.

"Afternoon, Nora." Larry, the butcher, leaned his sharp, pointy elbows on the white counter above the meat display. "Can I get you something?"

"Have you got any lox?"

"Lox?"

"Smoked salmon."

"Like jerky?"

"Not exactly."

"Hmm." Larry rubbed his chin. "Can't say we've ever had any lox. You're the first that's asked for it, to my recollection."

"So you won't be getting any in soon, I suppose."

"Probably not by the end of the week, no." Larry gave her a sheepish shrug. "How about some trout? That's in the same general category, at least."

Trout on a bagel. The dilemma of lox versus trout certainly helped put Balenciaga in perspective. "No, thanks anyway, Larry."

This time in Montana had given her many new perspectives on what was important in life. She hoped that when she returned to Hollywood—and deep down, in spite of all her delaying tactics and battles with Burke, she knew she'd have to, eventually—she'd be able to keep things like bumps and lumps and lox in their proper places.

BURKE SLIPPED a stack of faxes into his brief-case, saved his laptop files and shut down the ranch-house office computer as afternoon faded into early evening. He'd been able to cobble together a connection with Holly-wood, and he'd been able to gather quotes and information to plug a few more holes in his preproduction budget. Being forced to work without his folders and files, without a Los Angeles directory at hand and a conveniently organized space surrounding him had added several layers of frustration to his efforts.

His cell phone buzzed, and a glance at the

screen told him there was one more frustration to face. "Hello, Myron."

"How's the weather out there?"

"Sunny."

"And warm, I'll bet," said Greenberg with a disagreeable chuckle.

"Warmer than you'd think." If you were thinking of walk-in freezers. "Did you get my e-mail with the bids from the caterers?"

"Yeah, I got it. Are you making any progress with Nora?"

"Some."

"What kind of answer is that?"

"The truthful kind."

The silence that stretched over the next few seconds nearly hummed with hostility. "All right," said Greenberg at last.

"All right?"

"It's progress, right?"

"Right." Burke frowned. "Some."

"Better than none." Greenberg's cheerful tone was as unpleasant as his usual blast of invectives. "By the way, there's someone I want you to add to the company payroll. Casey Tomascheski."

Probably the whiz kid Fitz had warned him about. Burke opened his address file and tapped a few keys. "Male or female?"

"Female."

Of course. "And how does Ms. Tomascheski spell her name?"

He entered the correct information, including her e-mail address and phone number. And then his fingers halted, poised over the keyboard, when Greenberg supplied Ms. Tomascheski's work address. "That's my office."

"That's right," said Greenberg. "It's certainly been convenient, having one right there on the studio lot."

"What's she doing in my office?" Burke pulled his fingers from the keys and curled them into a fist. "I didn't request an assistant."

"I'm aware of that. Just like I'm aware of your exemplary work ethic and your concern for the company's bottom line."

An obnoxious little sigh punctuated Greenberg's sarcasm. "It seemed easier on everyone involved to take it on myself to provide you with the support you obviously need but never would have asked for. Support you deserve while you're slaving around the clock, in uncomfortable circumstances, for all of us back here at home. There'll be plenty of room for a second work space in that convenient studio lot location, once we get rid of the sofa and shove your desk against the wall."

Burke flexed his fingers and ordered himself to stay calm, to do or say nothing he'd regret later. "I don't quite know how to respond to your generosity."

"Don't worry about it. You've got enough on your plate as it is. I'm sure you'll find some way to thank me."

Greenberg shot off a list of duties and details Burke was to hand over to his new assistant, a list that removed all but one of his responsibilities.

"I want you to be free to concentrate on Nora right now," Greenberg said. "Easing your workload will give you the time you need to get that job done."

"I appreciate your efforts on my behalf."

"Anytime, Elliot."

Burke circled a finger lightly over the laptop's trackpad. "And what will Ms. Tomascheski's duties entail when I return from this business trip?"

"We can work that out later, when we see where things stand."

Burke ended the conversation and then stared at the phone in his hand, battling the urge to call Fitz. Greenberg would expect him to do exactly that—which meant the agent might be using Burke as a pawn in another pissing match with his partner. Burke didn't want to give him the satisfaction of playing that particular role in his game.

Or Greenberg had already secured Fitz's permission to pull this stunt. Perhaps Fitz had agreed—in a theoretical and noncommittal manner—that Burke needed more help, without suspecting that his partner would move so fast to turn a vague agreement into an uncomfortable reality.

Uncomfortable enough to maneuver Burke into handing in his resignation.

He rocked back in the creaking office chair, debating making a phone call to the young, attractive, ruthlessly efficient and ambitious Ms. Tomascheski. She was undoubtedly all those things—Greenberg wouldn't have chosen anyone else. Anyone less.

Instead, he wrote a brief, ruthlessly efficient e-mail and sent copies of the appropriate files to the whiz kid.

He needed a bit of distance, a bit of time to think things through. Time to make a few calls, to touch bases with a few contacts. If he weren't very, very careful during the next few days, he might very well lose his job to his new assistant. And though Fitz continued to assure him of his employment security within the production company, he preferred to keep things—his duties and respon- sibilities, his office and routine—as they were.

Fitz didn't want him to pressure Nora with business matters; Greenberg didn't want him to work on the budget. Neither of them wanted him to come back, unless it was with a signature on a certain piece of paper he wasn't supposed to mention. That didn't leave him with much to do but spin his wheels in his private version of a deep freeze.

Nothing to do but "concentrate" on Nora.

So that's what he'd do. He'd take her out to dinner tonight, and then they'd have a talk. He wouldn't have to discuss the contract with her.

She already knew what he wanted.

And as for wanting other things…

He slipped the laptop into its spot in his briefcase. Those other things gave him several more reasons to be very, very careful.

CHAPTER THIRTEEN

NORA LEANED AGAINST the nursery doorway in the Hammonds' ranch home, watching Maggie change Ashley's diaper on the changing table she'd purchased in Butte the weekend before. "Benita outdid herself tonight," said Nora. "That was the best *carne asada* I've ever had."

"She's been pretty bent out of shape lately, since Wayne and I have been eating so many meals at Granite Ridge." Benita, Wayne's feisty longtime housekeeper, made a habit of dishing out her thoughts and opinions along with her spicy cooking. "When Burke called and invited us to join the two of you for dinner in town tonight, she told us to be sure and bring another freezer back with us, because she's running out of room for all the frozen dinners she's been fixing."

"I'm glad you invited us to join you here instead, to help soothe her feelings." Nora ran a hand over her very full stomach. "Although I was surprised when Burke told me about the change in the dinner plans."

Maggie glanced at her. "I heard about the spaghetti incident."

"And the breakfast fiasco." Nora rolled her eyes. "I suppose he's trying to make sure he gets fed somewhere, since he hasn't had much luck at the cabin."

She wandered into the nursery to admire a miniature quilted wall hanging Jenna had fashioned. It featured stylized mountains and horses and incorporated the soft, natural tans and greens Wayne had used throughout his house.

The house was an impressive place, a soaring, spacious building of stone and wood and glass, built to mark his success after years of backbreaking labor reviving the ruined ranch left to him by his alcoholic father. Quiet, shy Wayne Hammond was as impressive, in his way, as the home he'd created.

She fingered a lampshade speckled with stars. "This is going to be a gorgeous room."

"Thanks," said Maggie as she snapped the last fastener on Ashley's pants. "Now that we know we're expecting a boy, I can add the finishing touches."

She picked up Ashley and hugged her close. "By the way, I ran into Burke when I was at the baby shop in Butte yesterday."

"You did? He didn't mention it." Nora pulled a cloth diaper from her tote, slung it over her shoulder and settled into the deep, comfortable rocker in one corner of the room. "You should see what he got for Ashley. It's this clever little ball with lots of fat holes for her fingers so she can actually get a good grip on it. It's her new favorite."

"Glad to hear it. I got one, too."

"Did you help him pick it out?"

"No, he helped me." Maggie deposited Ashley in Nora's lap. "He's done a great job with his research."

"Research?" Nora lifted the hem of her sweater to begin her nursing routine.

"He was discussing the hand-eye coordination benefits of that particular toy with the saleslady when I walked in."

"He probably found out all about it on the Internet." Nora shook her head with a smile. "Leave it to Burke to do market research on a gift for a baby instead of just getting something fun or pretty."

"Yes, imagine a man taking that kind of time and care with something so simple and straightforward." Maggie stared at her. "I can't believe you're not picking up on the signals here."

"What signals?"

"He asked me what I knew about educational toys for infants. Considering the fact that I'm a teacher from a large city who's planning on raising my child out here in the middle of nowhere."

Nora frowned. "I hope you weren't insulted. He probably meant well."

"He meant exactly what he said." Maggie pinned her with a meaningful look. "He wanted to know if there was more to caring for a baby than seeing to its physical needs."

"That sounds like something he'd say." Nora shifted Ashley. She was deeply touched by Burke's efforts in choosing an appropriate gift for her child but vaguely uneasy about the motives behind his questions. "What else did he want to know?"

"If there were exercises of some sort to improve the steadiness of Ashley's head."

"There's nothing wrong with her head."

"Don't get your back up." Maggie settled on the ottoman near Nora's feet. "He knew all about the development of small and large motor skills and the appropriate age ranges for each, according to sex. He said he just wanted to help her along as much as possible."

"Well, what do you know." Nora smiled at her daughter. "He is interested, after all."

"Oh, he's beyond interested. I think we're talking about total fascination here." Maggie fingered one of Ashley's curls. "Did you know he'd never held a baby before?"

"Really?"

"Had you? Before Ashley?"

"Once." Nora remembered a Christmas trip out of the city, the year the current nanny had taken a lonely eight-year-old to spend the holidays with her own family. "Only once. Only for a minute or so."

"Was it terrifying?"

"Completely." She leaned against the headrest with a sigh. "Gotta give the man credit for trying, I suppose."

"I've always given him credit for a lot more than that."

"What do you mean?"

"He put up with Kelleran all those years."

Nora laughed. "What is it with you and Fitz?"

Maggie smiled. "It's the sibling rivalry I always wanted, with a brother-in-law who makes the teasing worthwhile."

Her expression turned thoughtful. "And not only is Burke still working with Fitz, now he's dealing with Greenberg, too—who I understand is a piece of work."

"Greenberg's bark is worse than his bite." But it was a pretty nasty bark.

Maggie gave her a shrewd look. "Methinks you're doing way too much protesting here."

"About Burke?"

"Yes, Burke." Maggie leaned forward. "You've been shrugging off a lot of what I've been trying to tell you tonight. Makes me wonder why you're so tough on the guy."

"I'm not." She lifted Ashley to her shoulder for a burp, unsettled by her friend's latest observation. With all of them, actually.

"I think you are," said Maggie. "I think you've been using him as a convenient punching bag. And I think he's just been hanging in there, taking it, biding his time. It's been fascinating to watch."

"So glad we could provide the evening's entertainment."

"Don't go getting all pissy with me." Maggie poked her knee. "Spill. What's going on between you two?"

"Ellie didn't tell you?"

"You told Ellie something you didn't tell me?" Maggie poked her again, harder.

"*Ow.*" Nora flinched, and Ashley made a gooey mess of a burp. "You weren't there at the time."

"I'm here now. And I fed you." Maggie handed her a fresh cloth. "I know Ellie didn't feed you."

Nora had thought the tale would get easier to tell with time and practice. She'd been wrong. "He kissed me."

"All right." Maggie leaned back with a wide grin. "I'll bet it was a hot one."

"Off the scale." Nora sighed deeply, remembering. Wanting more of the same. "And why is it neither of you is upset by this?"

"He seems like a good man. Stable, dependable." Maggie shrugged. "You could do worse."

"I already did worse."

"Divorce happens," said Maggie with another shrug. "You can't let it spoil your outlook on the opposite sex forever."

"Don't worry," said Nora as she dealt with more of Ashley's spit-up, "I don't intend to."

"So…now what?"

"More of that punching-bag stuff, I guess," said Nora, "until we figure things out."

HOURS LATER, in the big bed in their shadowed room, Maggie skimmed her hand over Wayne's wide, muscular chest and smiled at the slight tremor beneath her fingers. "What were you and Burke talking about for so long tonight down in the cellar?"

"Wine."

"And?"

"Women."

"And?"

"That's about it."

"Come on, what else?"

"Song?"

She poked him, and his chest sank with a put-upon sigh. "What else am I supposed to say? Give me a hint, Maggie."

She shifted up on one elbow to glare at him. "Don't play that game with me, wise guy."

"I couldn't even if I wanted to. You never explain the rules."

She smoothed her hand over his chest again. "Just tell me everything he told you about what's going on between him and Nora."

"Nothing."

"Nothing's going on?" She circled one of

his flat nipples with her fingernail and smiled when he sucked in his breath. "Or he didn't tell you anything?"

He opened one eye and squinted at her. "Is that a trick question?"

"Playing for time?" She leaned down and nibbled on his lower lip. "I know that move."

He rolled toward her and trapped her legs beneath his. "You know this one?"

"I seem to recall that one, yes." She lay back and pulled his head to hers for a teasing, tempting kiss. "Mmm. Very nice. But not the kind of move I wanted to discuss right now."

"Can't it wait?" He nuzzled the sensitive spot behind her ear until her toes curled. "I've got a different kind of move in mind that doesn't need any discussion."

She sighed and trailed a finger over his shoulder. "I'm worried about Nora. I don't want to see her get hurt again."

"You think Burke is going to hurt her?" Wayne lifted his head with a frown. "They're friends."

"We were friends once."

"I was never your friend."

"We were friends in high school."

"Not really. I didn't move in your circle."

"When I came back, then. Last summer—

we were friends then." She ran a finger over his face, tracing the ruggedly handsome terrain. "And in the fall, when you were helping me with the stage project—"

"We were acquaintances back then. Friendly adversaries. And then we were lovers." He reached between them and spread his hand over the bulge in her abdomen in a soft caress. "And now we're parents."

She lowered her hand to place it over his. "Nora and Burke have been friends for a long, long time."

His hand stilled. "Then they need to be careful."

"I knew you'd understand." She twined her fingers through his. "A friendship between a man and a woman can get tricky when it shifts to something else. Something with a little heat."

He brought their hands to his lips and brushed a kiss over her knuckles. "Sounds like a recipe for a love affair."

"Or a disaster."

"Why don't you think it would work out between them?"

"I didn't say that."

"Seems to me they have a lot of things in common."

"But they go about them in different ways."

He pulled his hand from hers and tipped back her chin. They stared into each other's eyes, and she knew he was remembering, as she was, how their love affair got its start. "That's not necessarily a bad thing," he said.

"But it can be difficult."

"Is love ever easy?"

"It can be."

"Yes." He kissed her, slowly, sweetly. "Sometimes."

She lifted a hand to frame his face. "Most of the time."

"I'm glad you think so."

"I do think so. If two people are lucky. If they're right for each other."

"And you don't think Nora and Burke are right for each other?"

"I'm not sure." She sighed as he slid an arm beneath her to pull her closer. "He seems so...so stiff. Stiff and stuffy. Too stuffy, for her."

"He throws a mean game of darts."

"And that's supposed to make a difference?" She rolled her eyes. "Men."

"We bonded in battle. And in the cellar." He skimmed his fingers down the center of her, a long, tingling stroke that left silvery shivers in its wake. "I like him, Maggie. And he's Fitz's friend, has been for a long time. That counts for something, too."

"Yes," she said with a sigh, "I suppose it does. Damn it."

His quiet chuckle vibrated through her. "I love you, Mrs. Hammond."

"I love you, too."

He moved over her, sank slowly against her and wrapped her in a lover's embrace. "See how easy that was?"

NORA SLIPPED ASHLEY into her crib and made her way back to the front room to spend a few moments with Burke before heading to bed. The big dinner, the long visit with her friends and the cozy ride back to the ranch had left her relaxed and drowsy.

She found him in the kitchen, adding water to the kettle. "Tea?" he asked.

"No, thank you." She yawned and curled into her favorite corner of the sofa. "It's late. I'm going to bed soon."

"I've been wondering," he said as he put the kettle on the burner. "If you stay here, where will Ashley go to school?"

So, he'd decided it was time for Round

Two, and this time he'd chosen her daughter as a bargaining point. Suddenly awake and alert, she throttled back a hot spike of anger. "I know she's growing fast, but I don't think I have to worry about that for a few years yet."

"A very few." He reached into a cupboard for a mug. "Preschool can be an important part of a child's development."

"Did a little research on the Internet, did you?" She kept her smile light and friendly. "And now you're an expert."

"You don't have to be an expert to know about something as basic as preschool."

"If it's that basic, then I should be able to find a good one anywhere, right?"

"Perhaps." He made a slight adjustment to his glasses. "But what will you do about kindergarten? First grade?"

"I suppose we'll take it one grade at a time." She sighed and rubbed at the spot between her brows. Why did he have to start this discussion when she was so tired? She'd been in such a good mood and looking forward to…well, something more pleasant than this discussion. "There are schools in Montana, you know? I've met plenty of intelligent, well-adjusted people who attended them."

"I wonder how many of them would have been able to get into the better colleges if they'd wanted to attend one."

"College is more than a few years away."

"But it wouldn't hurt to start planning for it now."

She glared at him. "Why the third degree about Ashley's college plans?"

"I'm just asking you to consider the opportunities a place like Tucker can provide for a student versus those in a larger urban area."

"An area like Los Angeles."

"For instance."

"All right." She straightened on the sofa cushion, squaring off with his arguments. "So Los Angeles has more schools."

"And other educational opportunities."

"Which we can take advantage of when we visit."

"It would be much easier and much less complicated to let the school make use of those opportunities, don't you think?"

She stood and moved to the stove to toss in another log. "Are you implying that I wouldn't be able to provide a good education for my daughter in a place like this?"

"No, that's not what I'm implying." The kettle whistled, and he turned to make his tea.

"I'm simply suggesting that with all the educational opportunities and choices a larger city provides, it would be easier to find the resources to help you do that. And one of those resources could be an excellent school. A college preparatory school, if you choose to go that route."

"I don't have to choose any route tonight."

"But you do need to consider it."

She narrowed her eyes at his back. "You don't have to remind me of my parental responsibilities."

"Nora." His shoulders rose and fell with a deep sigh before he turned to face her. "I'm sorry. You're a wonderful mother. An amazing one, really. I'd say I'm a bit surprised by just how good you are at parenting, but that might get me in trouble."

"More trouble, anyway."

"As long as I'm in trouble already…" He calmly sipped his tea. "You have to admit, Tucker doesn't have as much to offer either you or Ashley as California does."

"Maybe I don't want what California has to offer anymore." She could almost feel him pushing her buttons, prodding her places she didn't want to go, and she knew she was too tired to do justice to her side of the argument.

But that didn't stop her from arguing, just for the sake of the fight. "Maybe I'm happy here in Tucker, so happy I want to stay and make a new life for myself and my daughter."

"And how will you support yourself and your daughter in this new life?"

"I don't know." She waved away that problem. "I'll think of something."

He raised his mug to his lips. "You have no skills but acting."

"I'm not entirely helpless," she said with a toss of her head. "Or unable to learn something new."

"Can you honestly see yourself as a clerk in some store? As a bookkeeper or a secretary?"

She narrowed her eyes. Though it was a valid question, one she asked herself a dozen times, it was hers alone to ask. "Why does it have to be a job like that?"

"It doesn't have to be."

He set the mug on the counter and folded his arms across his chest. "You have a chance for a wonderful career—a fascinating, spectacularly successful professional career. The kind of career most people dream of having for themselves. A career doing work you love with people who care about you—if only you'll come back to California."

"If I do," she said as she paced, "if I go back to that fantasy of a career, what kind of a life will that be for Ashley? A life with a mother who's a celebrity. A life in a fishbowl, ducking to avoid the paparazzi."

"You mustn't have been too concerned about that when you conceived her."

She gasped, stunned by the calm and quiet way he'd sliced clean through her. "What a hurtful, awful thing to say."

"You're right. I'm sorry." He pinched at the bridge of his nose and knocked his glasses out of place. "I seem to be apologizing quite a bit lately, and I'm sorry for that, too. For being so clumsy with this."

He met her gaze, and she knew him well enough to read every unspoken word of exhaustion and frustration and misery in his eyes. And every hint of despair between the lines.

"I never meant to hurt you," he said. "Or to offend you."

"No, I'm sure you didn't. I'm sure you haven't meant to offend me with any of the things you've said tonight."

She straightened her spine and wrapped her robe more tightly around her. "I suppose I'm partly to blame. I never should have let myself get caught up in discussing something with you that is none of your business in the first place."

She swept from the room, chin high and dignity intact, strode down the short hall and closed her door with a careful but decisive click of the lock. The exit had been one of her best—dramatic, yet subtle.

Too bad the end of the scene had broken her heart.

CHAPTER FOURTEEN

BURKE LAY COCOONED in a pile of quilts Tuesday morning, staring at the rough-edged beams and knotty planks and cobwebs and bits of resin on the ceiling of his cabin room, wondering how he was going to get through a workday with no work on the agenda.

No work other than a phone call or two. He planned to contact Ms. Casey Tomascheski at precisely nine o'clock Pacific time—and that introductory conversation wouldn't last more than a quarter of an hour, at most. He could call Greenberg and report on his conference with Casey—and once Greenberg discovered Burke wasn't contemplating either a resignation or suicide, he'd lose interest in the chat and disconnect.

He supposed he could call Fitz and report on…on how he'd upset Nora the evening before.

He squeezed his eyes shut. That wouldn't be pleasant.

He rolled to a sitting position and shivered as his bare feet came into contact with the icy wood floor. Before he called Fitz, he needed to get past the unpleasantness of facing Nora for the first time since their latest argument. Then he could relax and look forward to the lingering unpleasantness of this farce of a working vacation in this farce of a winter resort.

Through his door, he heard Nora's phone ring and the muffled sound of her voice as she answered it. He collected the clothing he'd need for his morning routine in the bathroom, looking forward to the heat of the shower.

He opened his bedroom door to find Nora there, with Ashley slumped against her shoulder and the phone in her hand.

"Fitz would like a word with you."

He took the phone from her, and she turned on her heel and marched back to her front room.

The unpleasantness was starting ahead of schedule.

NORA HAD ALWAYS FOUND IT impossible to hold a grudge. Her temper spiked hot and fast, and then faded away as quickly as it had flared up. Life was too exciting, too filled with wonderful people and interesting places, with holidays and celebrations and fun, to waste time dwelling on silly, petty things like misunderstandings.

Holding a grudge with Burke would have challenged a champion grudge holder. No one she'd ever met could play the role of the chastised, groveling man with quite the same touch of wobbly dignity, and she'd discovered she was a sucker for his unique interpretation of the part. Particularly since she'd been able to skip the distress of the chastising stage and move straight to the kiss-and-make-up part.

Without the kissing. She sighed over that missing element as she rinsed and stacked the breakfast dishes.

In the clean, clear light flooding through the kitchen window, their misunderstandings of last night shriveled to indistinct shadows. He'd misunderstood the level of her anger and fatigue and had pressed too far, too fast. And she'd failed to appreciate his concern for Ashley's welfare. Hadn't she been wishing, just a few days ago, that he'd show more interest in her daughter? And then she'd all but jumped down his throat when he'd done exactly that.

Over, done with, behind her now. But she wasn't the only one with a misunderstanding or two to sort out. It had been impossible to ignore the low, intense tone of Burke's voice behind his bedroom door during this morning's talk with Fitz. He'd left his brief-case behind when he'd come to breakfast, and he hadn't mentioned using the office at the ranch house.

She hoped there hadn't been trouble at work or a serious disagreement between her friends.

Behind her, the opening notes of a Vivaldi double concerto swirled through the front room. She hummed along and moved to the Baroque beat as she stacked the last of the dishes, and then she turned to see Burke with Ashley balanced on his arm, one of her tiny hands cupped in his. He stepped and swayed in time to the music, moving with the baby in his own version of her mother's dance.

Her chest constricted so swiftly, so violently, she had trouble drawing breath. They looked so beautiful together, so natural, their dark-haired heads tipped toward each other's and their expressions a matched set.

She had to force her words past a swelling spot in her throat. "What are you doing?"

"Teaching her to dance." He executed a reversal that put a smile on Ashley's face. "She's already quite good at it."

"A natural, hmm?"

"With an excellent sense of rhythm." He stopped suddenly and carefully dipped Ashley toward the floor. She gave him one of her hiccupy laughs, and he grinned and kissed her nose as he straightened.

Oh, my. Nora raised her hand to cover her heart, but it was too late. She'd already lost it to this solemn man with the baby spit-up on his sleeve.

"I don't think I've ever had a partner so willing to follow my lead," he said.

"So that's the appeal." She took a deep, shaky breath and joined the dance. "You wanted a woman who'd do whatever you suggest."

"Not necessarily." He caught her hand and pulled her into an awkward threesome. "It can be tiring making all the decisions about which way to turn, which opening to take. Which set to join or sit out."

"I thought men always wanted to be in charge."

"Of other men. With women, the appearance of being in charge is all we can hope for."

Nora rested her head against his shoulder. Ashley's tiny fingers grasped her hair and tugged. "Ken wanted to be the one in charge, and I tried to let him have his way. Maybe he didn't want it as much as I thought he did."

Burke stroked his free hand along her back. "Ken didn't appreciate what he had."

Ashley burped, and Nora pulled away, too late. "Aw, hon, look what you did to mama's hair. And Burke's shirt," she added.

"I'm sorry." He stopped and cleaned the baby's face with the diaper slung over his shoulder and then offered it to Nora. "I shouldn't have been dancing with her so soon after her breakfast."

Nora took the cloth from him with a disbelieving look. "You can make excuses like that for her after the past few days?"

He shifted Ashley higher on his shoulder and then lifted a hand to adjust his glasses. "Making excuses for a woman is one of a gentleman's most sacred duties in life."

She stretched up on her toes to press her lips to his in a brief, featherlight touch. "I'm not toying with you."

"I know." He caught her behind the head and pulled her mouth back to his for a quick, fierce kiss. "You couldn't, even if you wanted to. We have a very strict chaperone, in case you hadn't noticed."

He released her and took Ashley's hand, and the two of them danced away.

AFTER A DAY SPENT playing with Ashley and tamping his lust for Nora, after a difficult dinner at Walt's and a noisy drive back to the cabin with the colicky baby, Burke received a summons to the ranch house. He took Nora and Ashley with him in his SUV and followed them into the mudroom, a snug space filled with boots, jackets, hats, sacks of dog food and the aroma of Jenna's latest mouthwatering creation. He hung his jacket on one of the large hooks above a grubby bench and then took Ashley's carrier for a moment so Nora could do the same.

"You look as anxious as I feel," said Nora.

"Then you must feel like a condemned woman."

"It can't be that bad," she said.

"Yes, it can," said Fitz from the doorway. He leaned a shoulder against the jamb and slouched across the opening. "Hello, Nora. You're looking well."

"Thanks, hon." She brushed a friendly kiss across his cheek. "This is a surprise. I thought your shoot was scheduled through the weekend."

"I told them it was an emergency." His gaze stayed steady on Burke. "Hello, Burke."

"Hello, Fitz."

"What's everyone doing in there?" asked Jenna from the kitchen. "Come on out to the dining room. Nora, Burke, what kind of pie do you want? We've got chocolate silk and lemon meringue."

Fitz shifted to let Nora pass. "If you'll excuse us, Jenna, Burke and I are going to have a short business meeting. In the office."

"Oh, Fitz." Jenna tsked her disapproval. "Can't it wait until after coffee and dessert?"

"It won't take long." He led the way through a narrow, dimly lit hallway, avoiding the parlors and the rest of the family. Near the house's formal entry, he opened the heavy office door and gestured for Burke to precede him into the room.

Burke turned and waited as Fitz locked the door behind him. The actor curled one hand into the other and paced the length of the room, his steps muffled by a rug worn in a threadbare pathway by those who had paced here before him over the years.

"Are you going to punch me?" asked Burke.

"Not right now."

"Letting Greenberg do your dirty work for you, now that I've failed my assignment?"

Fitz stopped and slowly lowered his hands to his sides. "Maybe I will punch you after all."

"Go ahead." Burke raised one eyebrow. "That will give me a good excuse to hit you back."

Fitz scowled. "Then we'd both have to answer to Ellie."

"I'm not the one who's married to her."

"Damn." Fitz sighed and flexed his fingers. "I hate to lose before I get started." He resumed his pacing. "Maybe we should agree to just talk real tough and skip the stitches and broken knuckles part."

"Civilized, but not quite as satisfying."

"I always suspected you had a bloodthirsty streak." Fitz muttered a curse and shoved a hand through his hair. "How are things going?"

"As well as can be expected."

"That bad, huh?" Fitz shot a dark glance in his direction. "Have you kissed her again?"

"Yes. But…yes."

"But *what?*"

"Nothing."

"What do you mean, *nothing?*" Fitz stopped and raised a hand. "Never mind. Do you still want to?"

Burke had no intention of discussing this part of his life with anyone, and he pressed his lips together in a thin, tight line.

Fitz shook his head. "That's not good."

"I can't work like this, Fitz. There's no point in my staying."

"I hate to break it to you, but there's no other way. Nora trusts you more than ever now." Fitz gave him a hard stare. "And before you take a shot at beating the crap out of me for saying what I just did, let me finish."

Burke allowed himself to imagine beating the crap out of his best friend for a few satisfying moments, and then he tucked his hands safely into his pockets and gave Fitz a stiff nod to proceed.

"Listen. The fact that you're still in that cabin means a couple of very important things. Number one, you've managed to maintain a friendly basis for your relationship."

"We agreed nothing would change that. We want to remain friends."

"Wise of you both."

"But I'm not sure how much long—"

Fitz's hand shot up again. "Let me finish here. Number two, she probably wants you to kiss her again."

Burke opened his mouth to respond but changed his mind.

Fitz nodded. "I thought so. I didn't need to get much of a look at the two of you together to figure that one out. And I noticed she hasn't asked Will to fix the water heater in the foreman's place."

"Maybe she doesn't want to hurt my feelings. Maybe she doesn't want to kiss me and then toss me out like a piece of rubbish."

"Are you picking up on any rubbish signals?"

Burke frowned and shoved his hands more deeply into his pockets.

"I didn't think so," said Fitz with a grin. "So, buddy, what are you going to do about it?"

"About getting Nora to sign the contract and come back to California?"

"No. About kissing her again."

"That's none of your bloody business."

"Okay. That's cool." Fitz's grin widened.

Burke cursed under his breath.

Fitz's grin dissolved. "For what it's worth, I didn't know Greenberg was going to move Casey into your bungalow."

"But you did know he was going to put her on the payroll."

"I warned you something like that might happen."

"Warning me and telling me it's actually happened are two different things."

"Damn it, Burke, I've got better things to do than spy on Greenberg and report to you."

"You're right. I apologize." He stared at the carpet and willed his blood pressure to drop. "I don't think I've apologized so often in my entire life as I've done this week."

"You're on a roll, all right." Fitz leaned against the desk and crossed his arms. "And now it's payback time."

"I'm not leaving here."

Fitz froze. *"What?"*

"You're right. Nora trusts me, and I know what she needs. What she wants. I'm not leaving." Burke removed his glasses and rubbed at a speck. "Not until the contract issue is decided one way or another."

"I told you, I don't want you discussing that contract with her."

"And Greenberg told me to take a break

from my work on the preproduction budget."
Burke resettled his glasses on the bridge of
his nose. "It would appear my job consists of
doing nothing. As long as I'm doing nothing
in Montana."

"Greenberg doesn't know what's been
going on out here."

"And you don't know what's been going
on out there."

Fitz stared at the floor. "How did this get
so messed up?"

"Nora Daniels."

"That would explain it." One corner of
Fitz's mouth kicked up in a grin. "What's it
like living with her?"

"Remember what you said about payback time?"

"You love it—"

"No, I don't."

"—because you love her."

"I—" Burke blinked.

There was a knock on the door, and Fitz
walked across the room to unlock it.

Jody peeked in. "Wayne and Maggie are
here, and Gran says to come and eat your pie."

"We'll be there in a minute." Fitz kissed a
finger and pressed it to her nose before
shutting the door behind her.

He turned to face Burke. "Don't go all pale and weak-kneed on me now. I've got a job for you."

Burke summoned all his willpower to stay on his feet instead of sinking to the floor on those rubbery legs Fitz had mentioned. In love with Nora Daniels? He hadn't done anything bad enough to deserve a punishment like that.

Had he? Was he?

Yes, he probably was.

Damn. "What's the job?"

"You're back on personal-assistant status for the time being. As a personal favor," Fitz added.

Burke nodded. He was in no position to be offended, and Fitz knew it.

"I want you to prepare an itinerary for a holiday weekend in Los Angeles," said Fitz. "Plan for four—Ellie, Jenna, Jody, and one of Jody's friends. Probably Chrissy Fowler, but she can pick whoever she wants to take. I'll let you know the minute I've got her name."

"Right."

"Make all the arrangements—first-class plane seats, tickets to Disneyland, the VIP treatment at Paramount, dinner reservations, limo service, beach supplies. The works.

Call my service and have someone set up the Malibu house for company and put in some supplies. Someone to take care of the meals, if Jenna wants a break from cooking. Anything you figure that crowd will want to do—take care of the details so they can do it and I don't have to arrange for it." Fitz sighed and rubbed at his eyes. "I'm going to be working through most of the weekend to make up for the days here."

He resumed his pacing. "I'll pitch the idea to Ellie later tonight—it'll be a little tricky, 'cause I'll want to pull the girls out of school on Friday. But there's a three-day weekend with the Monday holiday, so it's a good time to get away."

"Jenna won't go."

"She will if she thinks Ellie needs help with the girls."

"I don't think—"

"I'll work on her, too. I'm not going to take 'no' for an answer this time." Fitz fisted his hand as he paced. "One more thing— transportation on the first leg. All we've got around here right now is a bunch of trucks, and you've got room in that SUV you rented to take four women and all their luggage to the airport in Butte."

"What about Nora?"

"She's not invited."

"That's not what I meant."

"I know what you meant." Fitz shot him a bland look. "You're not invited, either. You're going to stay here and look after Nora, 'cause Will's got his hands full with calving season, and we're currently a little shorthanded around here."

"Me?"

"Yes, you. You're already here, settled in that cabin. You know the routine, how to help with the baby. You're going to stay with Nora."

Burke shook his head in disbelief. "I don't think I realized until this moment how devious you could be."

"What do you mean? I've been trying to get Jenna and the girls out to Los Angeles for months. Don't you think they'd enjoy a break from the snow by spending some time on the beach?" Fitz swung his arms wide. "This is *perfect*."

"This has nothing to do with Jenna and Jody and Ellie. This is about Nora. You're systematically removing all her support."

"I'm not leaving her defenseless. I'm leaving her you."

"And who's going to protect her from me?"

"That oversized conscience of yours."

"Don't do this, Fitz." Burke swallowed the bitter lump of panic rising in his throat to beg again. "Don't do this to me."

"I'm doing you a favor. And when Nora signs that contract, Greenberg will think you're a genius. Hell, he'll probably give you a raise."

Burke straightened his glasses. "I'd rather get punched."

"Suck it up. This is your chance to be a real player." Fitz moved away from the desk and slapped him on the back. "Now, let's go celebrate the upcoming holiday weekend with some pie."

CHAPTER FIFTEEN

NORA STUDIED Burke and Fitz when they finally came out of the office, but she couldn't read anything in their expressions to give her a hint about what had happened between them. Burke looked a little pale and avoided meeting her gaze, but he ate every bit of his thick slice of chocolate pie and smiled over Fitz's tactic of using Valentine's Day as an excuse to overrule his wife's ban on gift giving.

He flustered Ellie by draping a gold chain with a flashing, heart-shaped ruby pendant outlined in diamonds around her neck, and thrilled Jody with a smaller version of the same necklace. He presented Jenna with a set of chocolate molds and candy-making supplies, he gave Ashley a bright red chewing ring, and everyone laughed when he handed Maggie a card with a picture of a skunk and a teasing verse.

"Nothing for me?" asked Nora.

Fitz pulled two boxes of chocolates from his duffel. "Hmm," he said as he stared at the second box with a puzzled frown. "I guess one of these must be for Wayne."

Maggie leaped from her seat and snagged the box from his hands. "Thanks, Kelleran. I'll make sure he gets some."

"Anything else?" asked Jody.

"What else could there be?" asked Jenna. "I've told you a dozen times, Fitz, you don't have to—"

"Give it up, Mom," said Maggie. "If the man thinks he can buy our affections with a few tokens, let's not disillusion him."

"You know what else I'd like?" Fitz winked at Jody. "Some fun in the snow."

"Tonight?"

"Sure." Fitz grinned at his family and guests. "Why not?"

"Because it's freezing out there," said Burke as Jody darted from the room.

"That's what makes the snow." Fitz headed toward the kitchen. "I'll explain the scientific principles to you later."

"Playtime." Maggie shook her head with a sigh. "Again."

Ellie stood and stretched, pressing her

knuckles at her lower back. "What makes you think it ever stops?"

"Sounds like fun." Nora bundled Ashley into her jacket. "I haven't played in the snow for years."

"I'll take her," said Jenna as she reached for the baby. "You go on out and enjoy yourself."

"What about you?"

"I'll be watching. Shoo," said Jenna with a little wave. "Go on, now."

Nora followed the rest of them—Wayne and Maggie, Will and Ellie and Burke—into the mudroom, where they collected their outerwear, and then through the door and down the back porch steps. Across the graveled parking area, at the edge of the porch lights' glow, Fitz and Jody shoved snow into deep, wall-like banks.

"Look, Mom," called Jody. "Forts."

"What do you think you're doing?" asked Ellie.

"Having a little fun." Fitz piled an armful of snow atop one of the fat, lumpy walls. "A little snowball fight."

"With forts?"

"Okay, a little war." He knotted a blue bandanna around a twig and stabbed it into the top of one of the barriers. "First team to capture the other team's flag is the winner."

"What do you mean, *capture?*"

"You know, *capture.*" Fitz began to tie a white napkin to another stick. "Go over to the other guy's fort and get it and bring it back."

"I'm on Fitz's team." Jody scooped up a handful of snow and patted it into a fat, messy ball. "You, too, Will."

He shook his head and shoved his hands into his pockets. "I'm too old for this kind of stuff."

"You're right. That's a definite handicap." Fitz shot him a wide grin. "That's why we get Jody."

"Yes." Jody made another ball and stacked it beside a growing pile of ammunition.

"Burke'll head up the other team," said Fitz. "He's big on organization."

Burke trudged dutifully to the other side of the yard.

"Who's on Burke's team?" asked Ellie.

"Hammond," said Fitz.

"Which one?" Maggie picked up a handful of snow and turned in Burke's direction, but Wayne snagged her by the jacket collar and she dropped her weapon.

"Come on," said Maggie. "I've been waiting for an opportunity like this."

Wayne shook his head. "Not in your condition."

She huffed her bangs out of her eyes. "I never thought I'd say this, but I really hate being pregnant."

"Come on, Hammond. Burke needs someone on his side." Fitz handed Jody the stick with the white flag, and she raced across the snowy field to hand it to Burke. "Home team versus the visiting squad."

Wayne swung his wife into his arms and lowered his mouth toward hers. "Kiss me goodbye, Maggie. I might not make it through alive."

She gave him a loud smack on the lips and shoved him toward Burke's fort. "Sorry, Ellie, but your husband is an idiot."

"You think?" Ellie grinned and looped her scarf around her neck.

Nora pulled on her waterproof gloves. "I want to know why Fitz is an idiot. This time."

"Maybe he forgot about Wayne's high-school sports career," said Maggie. Her smile was wide and wicked. "All-county quarterback. Three years in a row."

Nora laughed and jogged toward Burke's fort.

"Halt!" Burke held up a hand. "Who goes there?"

"Someone who wants to be on the same team as the local football star."

Burke glanced at Wayne. "Does Fitz know about this?"

"I don't know." Wayne caught a clump of snow with the side of his boot and shoved it into place against the inside of the low wall. "He's never mentioned it."

"He's never asked about my school days, either," said Burke.

Wayne and Nora stared at him.

"Cricket," said Burke as he adjusted his glasses. "I'm a rather good bowler, actually."

"Is that something like the pitcher in a baseball game?" asked Wayne.

"Yes." Burke picked up a handful of snow and squeezed it in his palm. "Now, all we need are some rules of engagement."

A clump of snow splattered across his jacket. Nora shrieked and dropped to her knees behind the fort walls. "I don't think Fitz is into rules."

Wayne swept a handful of snow into a quick ball and fired it at the other team, where it burst in a spray of white across Will's chest. Before he could launch another missile, Burke's well-aimed shot hit Fitz in the back of the head.

Fitz's suicidal assaults, Jody's sneaky

flank attacks, Will and Wayne's wrestling matches, Burke's attempts to bring order to the snowball chaos, Maggie's questionable coaching from the sidelines—Nora hadn't realized laughing so hard for so long could be so much fun or hurt so much. It doubled her over with spasms and robbed her of breath as she staggered back to her team's fort with an armful of stolen ammunition.

A crunchy blow landed across her shoulders, a second hit tipped her off balance, and she plowed into Burke and knocked him to the ground.

"Oomph."

He lay on his back, gazing owlishly at her.

"You lost your glasses," she managed to gasp.

"Yes." He blinked once, twice. "Nora, is that you?"

She choked back a giggle, and then she stilled. "I've never seen you without your glasses before. You have beautiful eyes."

"Thank you."

And a beautiful face. With no frames to obscure the angular slant of his cheekbones and the aristocratic slash of his nose, his features were surprisingly rugged. She'd always known he was an attractive man;

she simply hadn't been aware of the extent of his appeal.

Clark Kent minus the glasses. Desire punched through her, sharp and hot.

"I'd like to get up now," he said.

She rolled to the side, into the snow, and they both scrambled to their feet to hunt for the missing glasses.

"Here they are." Nora brushed as much snow from them as she could before handing them back.

"Thank you." He pulled them on, and a snowball smashed against the side of his face and knocked them askew.

"Time to come in," called Jenna from the porch.

"Aw, Gran." Jody patted more snow into a ball. "Just a few minutes more. *Please.*"

"Someone's hungry," said Jenna as she rocked a wailing Ashley. "And I've got hot cocoa to warm up the rest of you."

"Come on, Jody," said Fitz. "There are certain things in life worth quitting for. And your Gran's hot cocoa is one of 'em."

ON WEDNESDAY Burke woke early, energized by a sense of purpose. He showered and shaved and dressed in a white shirt and gray slacks, quickly kissed Ashley and Nora goodbye and headed to the ranch house for a breakfast meeting with Fitz before secluding himself in the ranch office.

He outlined his goals and organized his lists into various categories with dozens of items to check off as each arrangement was finalized. He was back in control, making himself useful, doing the kind of job he excelled at. The kind of job he could do for the film company, if only his bosses would give him his head. Give him their trust, and the authority to implement his talents.

He ate his lunch at his desk, to Jenna's disgust, absorbed in his work, plowing through the problems and dealing with the details. He printed the itinerary he'd created, added cross-referenced pages of alternate activities and various supplementary documents, loaded the thick stack into a large envelope and left it with Ellie to deliver to Fitz when he returned from his day spent assisting Will in the calving barn.

He drove back to the cabin in time to help Nora assemble a soup-and-sandwich dinner, and then he took a shift rocking the tired, crabby baby while her mother did the dishes.

It was all vaguely nine-to-five-ish and slightly domestic. Very nearly surreal.

NORA LEFT BURKE hunched over his laptop on Thursday morning and drove to the ranch house to show Jenna the baby sweater she'd finished knitting. She found her upstairs, in her airy, lavender-scented room, clothing spread over her bed and a suitcase propped open on a chair in the corner. "I can't believe you're going."

"Neither can I." Jenna held up two thick sweaters. "Which of these would be better for a day at Disneyland?"

Nora selected a lightweight cardigan from the articles on the bed. "You'll want something you can layer over a T-shirt and take off if it gets too warm."

"It's hard to imagine warm weather at this time of year."

Nora wiped a line of drool from Ashley's chin. "Are you going with Fitz?"

"Heavens, no. He left this morning, before light. The hours that man keeps…" She shook her head with a sigh. "He seems to thrive on his crazy schedule, though."

"He always has."

"And speaking of schedules," said Jenna,

her eyes bright with excitement, "you should see what he's got planned for us. A tour of the studio and a night at the theater. Shopping and beach time, too. It's going to be a whirlwind of a weekend."

Nora perched on the edge of the bed. "You'll have so much fun. All of you."

Jenna glanced at her as she folded a blouse. "I wish you were going to be there, too. I'd enjoy seeing your place."

"I'd enjoy showing it to you."

"Someday, maybe."

"Maybe."

Jenna settled next to her and stroked a hand over Ashley's head. "Any thoughts about when that 'maybe' might happen?"

"Not you, too." Nora sighed and nuzzled her daughter's cheek. "I've been getting plenty of subtle nudges from Burke. And some not so subtle."

"Are they working?"

Nora stood and slowly moved in her rocking step to the bay window alcove to stare at the rolling white fields threaded with silvered bands of cottonwoods and willows. "I know I have to go back, I've always known it. During all my time here I wondered about what I'd find there, and I worried that everything would be different. I loved my life before, and I didn't want to see it change."

She leaned her head against the lace curtain. "But now I'm worried that things won't be different at all. I want more than I used to have, and I don't want to settle for less. I just don't know how to make those changes happen for myself, how to make everything turn out the right way."

She straightened and faced Jenna. "Does that make any sense?"

"It does if I plug Burke Elliot into the parts you're circling around." Jenna cocked her head to the side. "I can see there's something there, something new trying to sprout up between the two of you. Something more than that friendship you keep insisting is the hard-and-fast definition of your relationship."

"But it's such a special friendship. A wonderful one. One I don't want to lose. Or ruin." Nora nuzzled Ashley's cheek. "What am I going to do about him, Jenna?"

"I wish I could help you figure that out. But I can't." She stood and slipped the blouse into her suitcase. "So I'm going to do the next best thing."

ONCE BURKE HAD DELIVERED Ellie, Jenna, Jody and Chrissy Fowler to the airport in

Butte on Friday morning, he decided he deserved an hour or two for himself. An hour with no excited chatter or endless giggling. An hour with no females.

Choosing to spend part of that hour in a baby store wasn't the wisest choice for avoiding high-pitched female voices. But he'd overheard Nora complain that she didn't have a hair bow for Ashley in a certain color, and he'd read an article on the Internet describing the benefits of exercises with a large, inflatable ball. He was eager to try it out.

A rack of decorated denim outfits caught his eye, and he fingered one of the dresslike tops. Very cute. What size did baby clothes come in? Size according to months in age— a sensible system. But how could he be sure what size Ashley wore? Was she appropriately sized for her age? He pulled one of the tops from the rack and held it up against his chest, estimating where Ashley's head would rest on his shoulder and where his hand would cup her bottom. The top seemed to be about the right size, and he placed it in his basket. As a designated uncle, he was allowed to splurge on small gifts.

He wondered if he should buy something

for her to wear beneath the top. And slippers—bootees, Nora called them. And what about those hair bows?

He made his way down another aisle, dropped a rainbow selection of tiny bows into his shopping basket and then snatched the phone vibrating in his pocket. He didn't recognize the caller's number. "Burke Elliot here."

"Hey, Burke." Will's soft voice was barely audible over the complaint of a cow in the background.

Burke's curiosity about why the foreman would be contacting him on his cell phone was immediately replaced with the realization that it must be an urgent matter, probably bad news. His fingers tightened around the phone. "What is it? Is something wrong?"

"No, everything's okay here, considering. We just brought another group of cows into the calving barn, and it looks like I'm going to be stuck here a bit longer than I'd anticipated."

"Have you heard from Nora?"

"Yep. Called her right before I dialed you, to get your number. She and the baby are doing just fine on their own. They manage to pull off that trick for a few hours every now and then, when they get the chance."

Burke's tension eased, and he fingered a

tiny nightgown with a drawstring at the hem and ducks waddling across the top.

"You might want to call her before you head through Tucker," said Will. "Check and see if she needs any supplies."

Burke added the nightgown to the rapidly growing pile of items in his basket and wished he'd chosen a cart. "I'd ask if you needed anything, but I imagine Jenna left you with enough food to feed a small army."

"You got that right. There's a lot of my personal favorites all wrapped up and ready to heat, since she's feeling so guilty. Nearly makes me wish she'd leave more often."

Burke tossed some duck-shaped footwear into the basket.

"Where are you?" asked Will. "Reason I'm asking is there's a winter-storm watch that went out about an hour ago. If you haven't started back yet, you might want to think about hitting the road soon."

"A storm watch?" Burke moved through the store, looking for the ball. "What does that mean?"

"Maybe nothing much at all. Too early to tell, really. It doesn't look that bad to me, but things can change quick around here. "

"I'm still in Butte, but I'm almost finished

with what I wanted to get done." He grabbed a ball and moved toward the register. "I can be on the highway in a quarter of an hour."

"That's fine. Didn't mean to worry you. Just checkin' on things, like I said."

Burke slipped the phone into his pocket. If there'd been no reason to worry, Will wouldn't have called.

On the other hand, if there were a genuine emergency, he wouldn't have let Nora stay at her place, alone with the baby.

Burke paid for the baby things and waited impatiently for the clerk to bag them. He pulled his phone from his pocket and hit the button for Nora's number on the way to his car.

Just checkin' on things.

CHAPTER SIXTEEN

TWO HOURS LATER, Burke slowed his SUV to a near stop as he squinted through the swirling mass of white, hoping for a landmark. There it was—the faint outline of the crooked black cottonwood stump that twisted over the creek bridge post.

He squeezed his fingers around the steering wheel and angled his car to the right, slowly, carefully, hoping his calculation of the arc of his turn and his estimation of the distance from the tree to the bridge weren't mistaken. If his math was off, his front fender was going to end up in the creek.

It had taken him nearly twice as long as usual to make the trip from Butte. The conditions along the highway had steadily worsened. By the time he'd arrived in Tucker, it was clear he couldn't chance stopping at the store in town—the snow was coming down so fast and thick he could nearly see it piling up in the road. And before he'd reached the entrance to Granite Ridge, the wind had taken that snowfall and turned it into a blizzard.

He'd heard the term blizzard before. He'd imagined the howling wind and the blinding white. But he'd never thought he'd be caught in one. And he'd never truly understood what the term *windchill factor* meant. The cold was a snarling, lurking thing, a beast with fangs and claws bared and ready to rake its way inside his lungs and shred his breath. Only the blast of the heater held it at bay.

The SUV bumped and slewed to one side, and the thought of icy water flooding inside made him brake, but he continued his slide down, down toward the creek. Too late to change his mind or his direction now.

Another bump, this one with a solid *thwump* beneath it. The bridge. He exhaled with relief and shoved at the hair that had fallen over his forehead, and then focused on the railing he could see near his door. He inched along the short span, preparing for the obstacle course waiting for him on the opposite bank.

He was desperate to make it to the other side, to Nora and the cabin. The alternative was to turn around—something he didn't want to attempt in the middle of the narrow side road—and head back to the calving barn to wait out the storm with Will and the crew.

He didn't want to consider the other possibility that Will had mentioned. The idea of wrapping himself in the emergency blankets in the cargo area and staying in this car through the night kept him moving.

Another jolt. The end of the bridge. Now a sharp turn to the left—no, not that sharp. He cursed and clenched his fists around the wheel as the car shimmied in the wind, threatening to tumble down the steep bank toward the streak of black water. He pulled out of it, bit by bit, angling toward what he hoped was the opposite edge of the road.

The front fender clipped something solid, and he adjusted his aim. His eyes burned with the strain of peering through the storm, with the effort of making some sense of the chaos of the world outside. Nothing but white in frozen barriers, white in slashing motion, white in a thick soup that threatened to smother him. In spite of the cold, sweat soaked the hair at his temples and trickled down his spine.

His head snapped forward when the car

collided with another drift, and he slumped in his seat to rest for a while, to take a few deep breaths and regain his composure. He'd begun to doubt he could make it any farther in these conditions. Even if he managed to back out of the drift and maneuver to one side or the other to pass it, he was having a hell of a time trying to figure out exactly where the road was. All the progress over the last half hour owed more to feel and guesswork than to any hint of a road.

The sky was darkening, the temperature dropping.

He picked up his cell phone and stared at it. He'd meant to help Nora by trying to make it to the cabin, not to add to her worries. But there was no reception here. If he couldn't move past this spot, he wouldn't be able to contact her and tell her that he wasn't going to make it, but he was safe.

As safe as a person could be stranded in conditions like these.

A branch broken from a nearby tree smacked against the passenger-side window like a gunshot. He glanced up and saw a light winking faintly through the milky gloom.

The cabin.

He eased the car into Reverse and tugged

the steering wheel to the side, aiming for the gap suddenly visible in the towering snowbank. The wheels spun, and the car lurched to one side before straightening. "Come on, you bugger," he said with a growl, "climb. *Climb.*"

Almost there.

The car bucked once, twice, and then fishtailed and rolled back several precious yards until the rear end crashed into a snowbank. He knew before he gave it a try that the car's wheels would spin without traction.

He'd reached the end of the road.

NORA MADE A TENSE CIRCUIT of the cabin's front room, swinging Ashley side-to-side with her swaying mother's dance step, trying to soothe them both. Each time she passed the wide window over the kitchen table, she'd try to peer through the wild, lashing snow. Sometimes she'd glimpse the bowed skeleton of one of the cottonwoods down by the creek, and sometimes she thought she could make out the boxy shape of her truck, already coated in several inches of white.

It was getting harder to see anything but the flurries flying past in a brutal, horizontal blur. It was getting dark.

There was no point in calling Will again. He was busy, literally up to his elbows in calving cows. And if he'd heard from Burke, he'd let her know.

No point in calling Burke again, either. Four messages were enough.

She checked her phone and proved to herself—again—that the connection was still working. So why hadn't he called?

Because he was somewhere his cell phone had no service. Somewhere he couldn't get to a land line connection.

Somewhere out there, trapped in his car, getting buried, freezing as he disappeared from view.

God, she hoped he was still in his car.

Of course he was. Will had told him what to do, and he had emergency supplies and a blanket. And more common sense, more calm and steady logic for dealing with a difficult situation than any man she'd ever known. He'd never do anything dangerous or foolish.

"So why doesn't he call?"

Ashley quieted a bit, and she shifted the baby to her shoulder, patted her back and started another meandering trip around the room. "It's just you and me, princess. We're going to have ourselves a big ol' slumber party—won't that be fun?"

She'd set emergency candles and matches throughout the house and filled containers with water. Now what? She should heat a bowl of soup and huddle with her baby in front of the television—to listen to still more talk of the surprising and sudden intensification of this winter storm to blizzard status.

Until the power went out.

She wasn't hungry and didn't think she could relax enough to get the soup down her throat, but she needed the nourishment, and she had to pass the time somehow.

She emptied a can of tomato glop into a saucepan and turned the burner to medium. Avoiding burned soup had been one of her first self-taught lessons. Maybe she'd—

The crash at the door trapped a scream in her throat. Snow gusted through the opening, and the vicious cold seemed to flay her, down to the bone. Ashley gasped and wailed.

"Burke." Nora wedged her howling daughter against the back of the sofa and tucked the throw over her before turning to catch Burke as he stumbled to the floor. He was wrapped in a blanket and caked in snow, clumsy and stiff, racked with violent shudders.

She was starting to shiver, too, fighting for breath as the cold swirled and sucked at her. She struggled to her feet and battled against the wind to shut the door. And then she fell to her knees to take him into her arms, ignoring the ice melting against her skin.

"Burke."

She had to get him warm, to peel that wet blanket from his body. Hot tears of fear and frustration streamed down her face as her daughter screamed on the sofa behind her, as her shaking, burning fingers clawed and dragged at his covering.

A sob escaped her when she saw what he'd held close to his body, buried beneath the jacket.

"Hold on, Ashley. I'll be right there, baby."

She jumped up and raced through the house, yanking the blankets and quilts from the beds. And then she knelt beside him again, spreading the bedding over the floor before shoving at him, grunting with the effort, trying to roll him to the center. *"Move,"* she said with a growl. "Help me out here, Burke."

He wobbled a bit, and arched his back, and she pushed and heaved and helped him flop over like a big, dark fish. His hands—oh, his hands were so white, like his face. She tucked his hands beneath his arms before she wrapped him in the blankets, covering him completely.

She threw another log into the woodstove and snatched her daughter from the sofa. "Shh, shh," she ordered them both as the baby's tears mingled with hers on her face. "It's all right. Mama's here. Burke, too. It's going to be all right."

AN HOUR LATER, with Ashley quieted for the moment in her mechanical swing, Nora tried again to get Burke to take some soup. She pressed a mug filled with it into his hands as he sat in the rocker near the stove. His teeth had stopped chattering, and there was some color in his face. She knelt beside him to loop her arms around his waist and press her face against the thick blanket wrapped around him.

His arm draped over her shoulders with a reassuring weight, and his fingers combed through her hair. "Am I forgiven?"

"This time." She lifted her eyes to meet his. "But if you ever pull a stunt like that again, I'm grounding you for life."

"I brought some things for Ashley."

"I found them." She'd wept a bit over the

giant ball and the pretty clothing—and those tiny, silly bows—and set them aside for later.

He stared into the flames behind the glass and slowly sipped his soup. She gazed at his face—his serious, beautiful face—and a world of emotions ping-ponged around inside her. Too many to identify, too many to process.

The timbers creaked and the windowpanes rattled as the wind slapped and spit at the cabin. The bitter cold pressed in, trapping them in the center of the fury, shutting them behind the whirling, deadly screen of blinding white. The storm's maddening energy pulsed through her, mocking her, daring her to break though and escape. She'd been through this before, earlier in the winter, and she detested this prickly restlessness, dreaded the slide into claustrophobia and the endless, sleepless hours of the night ahead.

She squeezed her eyes shut and hid her face against him, concentrating on the crackle and roar of the fire in the box, of the sensation of his fingers tangling in her hair and the lift and fall of his chest beneath her cheek. Burke would keep watch with her tonight. And tonight the restlessness, the prickle beneath her skin and the pressure on her heart, would center on him.

His hand stilled. "I've been thinking about why I tried so hard to get here."

"So have I." She withdrew from him and slowly sank to the floor. "You were a fool to risk it. I would have been fine without you."

His eyes were steady on hers. "Yes, I'm sure you'd manage quite well without me. There's a part of me that doesn't like it, but I understand why you feel you want to prove it. Why you have to prove it, to yourself."

"Don't say things like that." She rubbed her hands up and down her arms.

"I'm about to say several things you may not want to hear." He shifted to face the fire. "But if I don't say them, then that trip up the hill was for nothing."

"Tell me then. Why did you do it? Why did you come here?" She shoved to her feet, unable to remain still and bottle up those emotions at the same time. "You could have turned back to Butte. You could have stopped in at the barn or at the house. You shouldn't have kept heading in this direction when things got as bad as they did. And you *never* should have left the car. Damn it, Burke, you could have died out there."

"But I didn't." He took another sip and then set the mug to the side with slow, deliberate movements. "I told you, I could see the cabin lights from the road."

"And what if I'd turned them off?"

"But you didn't. And I'm here now."

He rose from the chair, shrugged the blanket from his shoulders and began to fold it in neat, square sections. "I've always been a great fan of following the rules. I've spent a lot of time trying to get others to follow the same ones so my life would be a tidy, orderly thing. I prided myself on being organized, on being thorough. For studying situations so I'd be better prepared to deal with all the variables. To be in a better position to take advantage of opportunities and to brace myself for the worst."

He tossed the folded blanket in an untidy mound on the rocker's seat. "But it seems I'm done with that life, for now at least. I realize that since I've been here, in Montana—practically from the moment I arrived—my tidy, orderly world has been turned upside down and inside out. And I've been helpless to deal with it, with any of it. Nothing I could have planned, or organized, or scheduled or arranged could have prepared me for the set of variables I've found in this place."

His eyes met hers, and what she saw there

pressed so hard against her heart she thought the weight might crush it.

"You see," he continued, "I've discovered that try as I might, with all my strength, I simply can't act—or react—the way I normally do. None of the old rules make any sense any longer. Not here. Not now."

He stepped toward her. "I want you to know why I took the risks I did to get here."

"You can tell me in the morning. When you've had some rest." She took his mug and crossed to the kitchen to rinse it in the sink. "We should both get some sleep."

"I wanted to see your smile, and Ashley's," he said. "I wanted to see them again. One more time, today, before I went to bed."

He closed his long, lean fingers around her arm. "I needed to see your smile. The need for it pulled me through the storm and brought me here."

The pressure in her chest was unbearable, and her eyes stung with the effort of drawing her next breath. She bit her lower lip to hold it steady. "I'd better give you one, then, so you'll go to your room and get some rest."

"I didn't explain it well enough. It's difficult for me to do. It's…"

He took her other arm and drew her close. "I want to be the one to put that smile on your face, Nora. I need that part of it, too."

"Burke." She pulled free to frame his face with her hands. "You do make me smile. I'm smiling right now, inside, where it counts."

"There's another part of it. Part of why I came back." He took her hands in his. "I want to make love to you."

"I want that, too." The words simply flew from her, before she had time to consider what she was saying, what she was doing.

The pressure and restlessness flew away, too. She curled her fingers around his. "It'll be—it might be messy."

"It's going to be messier than anything we could imagine. It's going to be the biggest mess either of us has ever made, the worst thing we've ever done. It'll be a monumental and genuine *disaster.*"

She smiled.

He tipped her chin up for a tender, yearning kiss. "I fought my way through a blizzard for that smile."

"Oh, my," she whispered. "I think that's the best seduction line I've ever heard."

"Then be sure to keep it in mind when I

make my big move." He took her hand. "Come to bed with me, Nora. Let's wreak havoc on what's left of our lives."

CHAPTER SEVENTEEN

HE WAITED—through a shower to banish the last of his chills, for Ashley to drink her fill and drift to sleep, for Nora to slip into her best silk gown and pin up her hair. They'd had their moments of mindless passion and reckless foreplay on the kitchen table, five days ago. Now they'd take their time with what came next.

As Burke entered Nora's room, he summoned all his control, all his self-discipline. He wanted to be very, very careful with this. With her.

He'd taken a lot of time to consider every aspect of this important step in their relationship, every angle of the process of making love with her—the seduction, the mood, the setting, the foreplay, the positions, the moves, the aftermath. What he hadn't considered were his feelings, and hers. He couldn't have imagined the enormity of what was welling up inside him. What he hoped was swirling through Nora, too.

He hadn't realized what was happening, as he'd moved toward this moment. He hadn't understood, until he'd reached this point, that the act of making love would be his way of expressing it.

He hadn't considered how he could possibly manage such a thing, how he could possibly communicate what he wanted her to know, and it troubled him. "Nora, I—"

"Shh." She moved to him and placed her fingers against his lips. "It's all right. We'll be all right."

And so it began, with shared smiles and a gentle kiss pressed against her palm. Another to her wrist. A fleeting awareness of the scent she'd dabbed there, something faintly floral. His new favorite.

Soft, so soft—the silk of her hair as it tumbled into his hands, the glide of her gown from her shoulders, the skin beneath his skimming fingers, the sigh rippling through her, the floating, fluid sensation of the moment as he pulled her into his embrace and reveled in her lush, womanly form.

He paused to light a candle at her suggestion, and the room's shadows flickered and faded as he turned to guide her down to the bed. Slowly, he reminded himself as he trailed a path of kisses down her neck, savoring her taste. Steady, he told himself as he shuddered beneath her lingering touch.

What a miracle, this pulse beating beneath his lips, this breath brushing across his ear, this hand smoothing over his chest. Nora, his friend. This beautiful, strong, talented, loving woman returning his secret smile, circling her arms around his neck when he pulled her close, twining her legs with his. Drawing him to her, wanting him as much as he wanted her.

Oh, how he wanted her. He strained toward her, needing desperately to make her feel, to make her aware of all that was inside him. He feasted on her mouth and devoured her with his gaze, chaining his greed to focus on her response. But her sighs and moans, her busy hands and her arching hips were too tempting, and he could feel his control slipping, could feel himself falling, sinking into the drenching pleasure of the moment.

He slipped inside her, and they froze and stared and smiled together, and then they began to move. Up-down, rise-fall, kiss-sigh, creating their own steps in their lovers' dance. Faster, deeper, richer, their silent music flowed around them, until they clasped their hands and took each other where they'd both longed to go.

Later, in the candlelight, he watched over her as she slept, stroking a fingertip through her hair. He wanted to savor this moment, too, to treasure this new miracle. She'd be the last thing he'd see before he closed his eyes and the first thing he'd see when he woke. Nora, his lover.

DEEP IN THE PREDAWN HOURS, Nora lay on her side beneath several layers of quilts, facing Burke, Ashley between them. Burke had dragged her mattress to the front room, and they'd fashioned a bed on the floor near the woodstove for added warmth. Candlelight cast its wavering glow across the honey-toned wood of the floor and walls and ceiling, and the sweet tenor of a Bach violin concerto rose from the corner where Burke had set the CD player.

He'd watched her while she'd nursed, and his smiles at Ashley's greedy gulps and contented sighs and whoops had helped banish her initial shyness. Now they cuddled and stroked the baby as she drifted back to sleep.

Burke gently brushed Ashley's hair from

her forehead with a fingertip. "Do you ever think of having another child?" he whispered.

"All the time." Nora raised herself on her elbow and rested her cheek on the palm of her hand. "I don't want her to be an only child. Like me."

Burke stared at the baby, silent and solemn. "I was an only child, too."

"I didn't know that." There were so many things she didn't know about him. Had never thought to ask, or felt that she could.

Now they had what remained of this night—and all the days and nights the storm might rage beyond this snug cabin. "Tell me about it. About your parents."

"They were busy people with busy lives. Older than most parents, I suppose, and settled in their careers. Consumed by them, really."

"I don't want to be that way. I want to put Ashley first."

"Then you will."

He skimmed a finger along the baby's forehead, down to the tip of her nose.

"Tell me something else," she said. "Tell me the first thing you remember."

"I don't know what that would be. I was—"

He broke off and looked at her, and a terrible sadness shadowed his dark eyes.

"I remember I was sitting at the dinner table," he said. "With them—with my parents. I knocked over my milk glass, and my mother rang for the cook to take me to the kitchen. She didn't even pause in the middle of whatever she was saying to my father, didn't look at me. She just picked up the little bell by her plate and rang it."

His gaze was focused on something other than the baby between them. "I remember the bright lights made the food on my plate look cold and greasy, and I wasn't hungry any more. And then I couldn't see the food, because I was crying. The maid scrubbed at my tears with a warm, damp cloth before she used it to wipe the counters." He glanced up. "I was banished from my parents' table for a year."

And he'd become a man who neatly aligned his things with other things. A man who took great care to organize his life and the lives of others, to keep everyone and everything in its proper place.

She reached across Ashley and trailed her fingers down his cheek. It was rough with dark stubble. "I don't want Ashley's first memory to be something painful. Something I caused."

"All you can do is try. And hope."

"I have to take her to the doctor's office on Tuesday for her first shots. I know she won't remember the trauma, but I'm not sure I'll recover."

"I'll take you. I'll be there for the both of you." He captured her hand and pressed her fingers to his lips.

She took a deep breath and exhaled on a long sigh. "Tell me more."

"My mother left my father when I was eleven. I came home from my first school term, and she was gone."

"Just like that?"

"Yes. My father summoned me to his library to inform me of the news, and then told me to change out of my uniform and into the clothes the maid had set out on my bed. He took me to my grandmother's house for holiday. For every holiday. Sometimes he stayed, too. Most of the time he didn't. He didn't get on well with his father."

"What did he do—your father?"

"He was a surgeon. A very good one, very involved in hospital affairs. Not much time for raising a son."

"Were you lonely?"

"Only on the holidays, when I missed my

mates." He bunched his pillow beneath his head. "Were you? Lonely?"

"Sometimes."

"Did you have schoolmates?"

"I changed schools a lot. That made it hard to make friends and keep them."

He stared at Ashley. "Where are you going to send her to school?"

"I'm not going to 'send' her anywhere."

"That's not what I meant."

She shifted to her back, careful not to jostle the baby, and turned her head to face him. "I don't know. I've got a few years to think about it."

"She's growing so fast. She'll look completely different when I see her again." His bleak gaze met hers. "She won't remember me."

"Babies this young don't remember anyone."

"She won't know about this. This—this time we had together."

"We could tell her."

"It won't matter. It won't be her memory." One corner of his mouth twitched in the ghost of a grin. "At least I won't be a glass of spilled milk."

"She'll know you love her. She'll feel it."

She swallowed against the burning knot in her throat. "You do love her, don't you?"

"Yes." He stared at her baby in his solemn, intense way. "Of course I do. Who wouldn't?"

And then his gaze shifted to her, that same solemn, intense gaze that sent liquid longing through her. He rose from the mattress, carefully lifted the sleeping child and laid her in the portable crib near the woodstove and then extinguished the candle before rejoining Nora and taking her into his arms.

She knew, in the gentle glide of his hands over her skin, in the heated kisses that skimmed along her body, in the urgent caresses that bowed her against him with her first release, in the frantic press of his mouth against hers, in the thrilling moment that he lost control and surged inside her, that he loved her, too.

Of course he did. She could feel it.

BURKE WAS AWARE that Saturday had somehow bled into Sunday, though he hadn't paid much attention. He and Nora had weathered the storm in their makeshift bed—for the mutual warmth, they'd agreed with knowing smiles. Brief forays to the kitchen for snacks of toast and scrambled eggs and soup, showers shared during Ashley's naps, playtime with the baby and the occasional checkin' in call from Will—these were the only markers punctuating the long, luxurious hours of love-making and sleep entwined in each other's arms.

Time had passed in a limbo of their own making.

AFTER TAKING HIS TURN at diaper duty—and indulging in a session of nibbling on baby toes—Burke scooped Ashley into his arms and turned to find Nora frowning at the television. On the screen, a toothy blonde perched on a tall stool, chatting with a man in spiky hair and a leather jacket. Behind them, photos of Nora and Fitz formed an oversized backdrop.

"What's this about?"

Nora held up her hand to silence him, and he listened to a fictional account of her blizzard ordeal. A secluded cabin, freezing temperatures, near starvation, a desperate attempt to keep her baby alive.

And through it all, a sizzling affair with the man likely to be producing her next film.

The scene behind the commentators switched to a slightly grainy shot of Burke

"I want an answer."

"Then I suggest you ask a different question."

"You're sleeping with her, aren't you?"

"That's not the right question, either."

Greenberg launched into a vicious tirade, and Burke slowly lowered the phone to its stand.

"You shouldn't have cut him off like that," said Nora.

"I don't want him teaching Ashley bad manners."

As he pulled Nora close to kiss her cheek he wondered who else had been watching that show—and what might happen as a result.

ELLIE SIPPED her glass of milk on Sunday evening and squinted at the rainbow sherbet colors spreading over the Pacific. Beyond the living-level balcony of Fitz's Malibu house, Jody and Chrissy raised their short boards over the frothy tumble of a wave, headed out to hitch another ride in the surf. Closer in, a real-life ad for one of those body-building machines she'd seen advertised on television jogged along the shore.

"Isn't that a picture?" Jenna sighed and stretched along the length of a wooden chaise lounge. "Sunset puts on quite a show out here."

"That's the only way it'll get noticed, considering the competition from the neighbors."

"Neighbors?" Jenna's gaze shifted toward the shoreline. "Oh, my. I see what you mean."

"Not that we don't appreciate the competition we've got at home."

"No, indeed." Jenna tipped down her sunglasses and watched the stranger jog into the shadowy rear entrance of a nearby mansion. "We've got enough to keep ourselves completely satisfied. It's just nice to remind ourselves of that fact with a little comparison shopping every once in a while."

Ellie smiled and set the empty glass on one of the fanciful iron-and-glass tables scattered across the expanse of the deck. Jenna had balked, at first, at making this trip— mostly because she didn't want to leave Will for so long—but it hadn't taken her more than the length of the flight out west to fall under the sybaritic spell of a Southern California holiday, Hollywood-style.

Limousine rides, elegant meals, dazzling shopping, VIP treatment—Fitz was pulling out all the stops to make this weekend one to remember. When Ellie had questioned the extravagance, he'd tugged her into his arms and donned his mournful puppy expression, begging her to give him this one chance to impress his mother-in-law.

The same way he'd begged her to let him give Jody a once-in-a-lifetime treat the last time he'd flown them out here.

Jody's laughter rang out over the rushing roar of a wave as she flailed through the water after her runaway board. Guess some once-in-a-lifetime experiences were meant to come around several times.

Behind her, through the slice of glass door open to the evening breeze, Fitz's voice rose with a touch of exasperation.

Jenna's lips pinched together in a disapproving pucker. "Sounds like things aren't going too well back home."

"He might be talking to Greenberg."

"Nasty little man."

"No competition there."

Ellie settled against the pillows at her back and closed her eyes. She didn't mean to eavesdrop on Fitz's business, really she didn't. But the snatches of one-sided conversation she overheard made her wonder what her husband was up to.

He'd told her he'd sent Burke to Montana to rush Nora out of the guest cabin and back to Hollywood. As fast as possible. And Fitz wouldn't do something like that unless he thought it was in Nora's best interests.

The door closed behind her with a quiet click. A suspicious click.

"Do you mind keeping an eye on the girls?" Ellie rose and collected the empty glass. "I'm going inside."

"They should probably come in soon, too," said Jenna. She visored her hand above her eyes and gazed at the scene below. "It's nearly dinnertime, and they'll need to wash up before they eat."

Ellie slipped through the door and glanced at Fitz as she made her way to the curving kitchen raised a few steps above the vaulted great room. He winked at her as she passed, but then he turned slightly to one side and made a quick and quiet end to the conversation.

"That was Burke," he said.

"I thought so."

"They survived the blizzard."

"They're both capable people."

"He'll only have to put up with the situation a little while longer."

"How much longer?"

"I don't know exactly." Fitz scrubbed a hand through his hair with a considering frown. "It's complicated."

"Is it?"

"Very."

She crossed her arms and gave him a steely-eyed look. "Try me."

"Now, Ellie, you don't want to discuss business in the middle of our nice vacation, do you?" He climbed the steps to the kitchen and rinsed her glass in the sink. "I brought you all the way out here to get away from all that."

"Just like you sent Burke all the way out to Montana to take care of all that. Or so you said."

"I did say it." He rubbed at an invisible spot on the speckled-stone counter. "That's why he's there."

She clamped her hand over his on the counter and gave it a warning squeeze. "What's going on, Kelleran?"

"What do you mean?"

"Believe me, you don't want to make me spell it out."

He stared at her for a minute, and she could see the wheels turning while he tried to figure out just how far he could push her—or how much he could hide.

"And you don't want to get smart with me, either."

"Now, hon, you know I know better than that." He pulled his hand from beneath hers and tickled his fingers up her arm. "I learned that lesson long before the honeymoon."

She brushed his hand away. "It didn't take very well, did it?"

He slipped his hands into his pockets. "What do you want to know?"

"Why is Burke in Montana?"

"To talk Nora into signing a film contract. That's goal number one. And if he can get her to move back to California sometime soon, that's a plus."

"He could have done that over the phone. No one's better on the phone than Burke. And he hates Montana."

She sucked in her breath as the reality of the situation hit her. "You know that. And you used it. You dragged him out there— dragged your best friend all the way out to a place he detests, just to make him miserable, so that Nora would take pity on him. So that Nora—another poor, manipulated friend of yours—would be put in the uncomfortable position of having to sign some piece of paper just to put Burke out of his misery."

"Now, hon, it's not as bad as—"

"No, knowing you, it's worse." She narrowed her eyes. "I wouldn't put it past you to have cooked up that whole water-heater scheme with Will."

He may have been a world-class actor, but he was her husband, and she was primed to catch the tiny shadow of guilt that flickered across his features. "Kelleran, I swear, I ought to—"

"Now, hon—"

"Don't you 'now, hon' me." She shoved her hair back from her face and paced to the giant stainless steel refrigerator and back. "You brought Jenna out here to get her out of the way, didn't you?"

"She seems to be enjoying her vacation."

"That's not the point."

"Why can't it be the point, if it makes her happy?"

Ellie slapped a hand down flat on his fancy counter. "This isn't business. This is personal. And if it's personal, I want to know what this is about. I need to know. I care about these people, too."

He stalked down the stairs to peer through

the tall doors overlooking the ocean. Jenna's lounge chair was empty; she must have gone down to the beach to call the girls in.

Fitz turned to face her. "He's in love with her."

"Who?"

"Burke."

"With Nora?"

Fitz nodded. "He's been in love with her for years."

"He told you this?"

"No."

"Then how do you know?"

"I've always suspected it. There were some major signs last summer, during the location shoot. And when she left..." Fitz shifted his shoulders in something shy of a shrug. "He hasn't been the same since she left. I thought if he went out there and saw how she's settling in, how—"

"How happy she is."

"She's not really happy."

"Then she's giving a damn good imitation of it, 24-7. I knew she was a talented actress, but that seems a bit extreme, even for her." Ellie tossed up her hands. "I can't believe you're doing this. Playing God with these peoples' lives."

"That's not what I'm doing."

She pointed an accusing finger at him. "Explain the water heater."

"I didn't have anything to do with that. It was a great idea, though—wish I'd thought of it."

Her lips twitched at his obvious dismay. "You did the same thing to Maggie and Wayne, didn't you? That's why you refused to fund her stage project last fall."

"I did fund it."

"Not until after you were sure they were going to get together."

"If I'd handed over the money when she asked the first time," he said patiently, "why would she have needed to go to Wayne for it?"

"And now you've arranged for Burke to be stuck in a sticky situation with Nora."

"They can both get unstuck any time they want to."

"That's not the point."

He threw up his hands. "Why is that important?"

"Because you can't go around meddling in people's private lives."

"I don't make a habit of it."

She fisted her hands on her hips. "How can I be sure of that?"

He gave her one of his famous grins. "You can't."

She knew she should be angry. She knew she should teach him a lesson he'd never forget. But his unrepentant glee in the face of her worst suspicions—and that killer charm of his—simply undid her.

Again.

She sank onto one of the counter stools and lowered her head to her hands. "What am I going to do with you?"

He dropped his gaze to the floor and scuffed at the rug. "I suppose you could tell me I'm a very bad boy and punish me later."

CHAPTER EIGHTEEN

BURKE WATCHED Nora push Ashley's neon pink stroller down a ghostly Tucker sidewalk, the wind rippling her long, trailing skirt around her shapely ankles and bare feet. A tall, faceless cowboy tipped his black hat at her as he passed. He leaned too close, much too close, and plucked the baby from the stroller.

The wind rose, scattering fat pink snowflakes and sending Nora's skirt swirling over the scene. And when the gust died, the stranger was gone, and Ashley, too. Nora screamed, and the sound ripped through him, but he couldn't move his feet, couldn't chase after the tall, black ghost as Nora sank to her knees in the pink dust, sobbing behind her hands.

He couldn't breathe, couldn't suck in the air he needed to set loose the scream in his mind, couldn't bear the crushing pressure and pain.

His eyes opened to the dark and his throat

ached with the remnant of a moan. He rolled to his back and lay with his arm over his face, waiting for the panic to subside and for his stomach to quit its shuddering roll. Just a dream, he told himself. Just a dream. He was in the bed they'd reassembled in Nora's room, and she was warm beside him, and Ashley was safe in her crib.

Ashley. The thought of her caught at the jagged edges of his heart and tugged him toward her, just to stare down at the curve of her fat cheek outlined in moonlight, to watch the rise and fall of her chest and listen to the sound of her baby breath. To reach out and brush at the curl on her forehead, so gently she'd never know he'd been there to worry over her in her sleep.

The dregs of the dream still clawed at him, and he knew he'd never forget that breath-robbing fear, that searing grief in the moment of loss. How could he bear to let her out of his sight? How could Nora? And yet they'd have to, over and over again.

"Burke." Nora rustled in the bed behind him.

"It's okay." He straightened, but he couldn't take his eyes off the baby. Not yet. "She's okay."

"Of course she is."

Nora rose from the bed to circle his waist with her arms. "Come back to bed."

"I had a dream. A nightmare, actually. It was—"

He didn't want to distress her, but the pain was too awful to hold inside, to keep to himself. He grasped for her hands where they rested against his stomach. "It was about Ashley."

She pressed her lips to his shoulder. "I've had those dreams, too. Awful, horrible dreams. The worst nightmares imaginable."

"How do you get over them?"

"I don't." She sighed, and her breath flowed over him and began to warm him. "But then she smiles at me, and it helps me forget how much they hurt."

He turned in her arms and cradled her face in his hands. "You're the most beautiful woman I've ever known, inside and out." He brushed her lips with his. "Come back to bed and let me try to show you how beautiful you are to me."

Beyond the kitchen window, miniature avalanches slipped from one tree branch to another as Nora chatted with Will on Monday morning. Foaming clouds scudded across a milky sky, and the jagged mountain peaks seemed to shred their edges as they passed.

"Will's going to work his way toward us with the snowplow," Nora told Burke as she disconnected. "He should be here in a couple of hours."

"I hope I can get my car started." Burke sat with his long legs stretched over the floor on either side of Ashley. He helped her sit up and handed her the honeycomb ball he'd given her, waiting for her to work her fingers through the spaces and grab it. "I'm supposed to go to Butte tonight and pick up Ellie and Jenna and the girls. I won't be back until late."

"I'll leave the lights on for you."

He gazed at her, and she knew he was wondering, as she was, how many more minutes they had together before the reality of the outside world came crashing in to shatter this precious interlude they'd shared.

There were still so many questions to ask, so many things to discover about each other. So many things to say.

He rose from the floor and carried Ashley and her ball with him to settle beside her on the sofa. "Have I ever told you know how much I adore seeing you on a movie screen?"

"No, you haven't." She curled her legs beneath her on the cushion and leaned against his shoulder. "Go ahead. And don't leave out a single detail."

He gave her one of his rare smiles, the one that made the grooves on either side of his mouth deepen and his deep-set eyes shine. "You take my breath away," he said. "All you have to do is look into the camera, and I couldn't look away if my life depended on it." He picked up the ball Ashley had dropped and held it for her to grasp again. "And it doesn't matter if thousands of other men are sitting in hundreds of other movie theaters, thinking what I'm thinking, because in my imagination, you're really looking only at me."

His smile faded. "That's an amazing quality, Nora. Not every actress can pull that off."

Something about the look on his face and the steady support of his warm body against her back helped her confront what she'd been hiding from herself for so many months. She drew in a deep breath and let it out on a long, shaky sigh. "I'm tired, Burke. So tired. I don't know if I can pull that off again."

"Of course you're tired. You're dealing with a baby and housekeeping chores and a houseguest who is making demands of his own." He leaned away from her to wipe spit-up from Ashley's chin. "But if you decide to give it up, I can console myself with the fact that I'll always have you on video."

She straightened and smoothed her robe over her knees. "I suppose people will stop renting those."

He nodded soberly. "The public is fickle."

"Even if I weren't so tired, even if I were rested up and back in shape and ready to work again, I don't know if I could do it."

"Are you afraid?"

The fact that he knew her so well and saw so much—and that his voice held nothing but concern—didn't make it any easier to admit the truth. *"Yes."*

"Of what, exactly?"

"That it was all a mistake. That whatever I had, whatever it was that I could do, was some kind of magic trick, an illusion I won't be able to repeat. Maybe if I studied again, took some more acting courses—"

He shook his head. "And learned to be like everyone else."

"It's a craft."

"Yes, I can see that part of it is." He shifted a fussing Ashley to his shoulder. "But part of it, the best part of it, is what simply pours out of here." He rested his palm over Nora's heart. "I imagine that's what makes you so weary—turning yourself inside out so that people like me are mesmerized. If it's a magic trick, it's one no one else can do. And nothing anyone can teach you."

She placed her hand over his. "You make me want to try to do it again. For you."

"That's not a good enough reason. It never was." He twined his fingers through hers. "You have to want to do it for yourself, too."

"And for Ashley."

"Ashley needs your love, not a part in considering your film roles."

"But they'll affect her."

"Yes, to some degree." He passed the baby to Nora. "But any job you take will have some effect on her. Any mother's job affects her children."

"You're right." She nuzzled her daughter's nose. "And you're right about what you said before."

She blinked at the tears stinging her eyes. "I wasn't concerned enough about how my career might affect her when I decided to get pregnant. I just wanted a child so very, very much. I didn't know how much I'd love her.

I couldn't imagine how it would feel. I only thought about what I wanted, what I needed. And now the way I feel, about her, makes me so afraid."

"Shh." He slid an arm around her shoulders and drew her into a sloppy three-way hug. "It'll be all right."

"How can you be sure? How can I?"

"Because you love her so much. Because you're afraid to do the wrong thing." She felt him kiss the top of her head. "It's not a bad thing to be afraid, I don't think. It's a human thing."

"Are you ever afraid?"

He sighed and hugged her closer. "Nearly every moment."

BURKE CELEBRATED Will's arrival with an invitation to join them in what he hoped would be the last tomato-soup-and-cheese-sandwich lunch for quite some time. After the foreman's departure, he left Nora nursing her drowsy baby in the bedroom rocker, rolled up his sleeves to deal with the kitchen chores and started a mental list of the groceries he'd purchase in town. Thick steaks, fresh fish, fat potatoes, salad greens, bottles of wine—

The phone rang, and he quickly rubbed a towel over his sudsy hands before snatching up the receiver. "Hello?"

"So, it's true."

Burke froze at the sound of Ken's voice. Until this moment he hadn't given enough consideration to how he might deal with Nora's ex. Now the reality and ramifications of the situation slammed into him, nearly knocking him to his knees. "What's true?"

"There's a rumor going around that Nora's taken up with someone new. Never figured you for that kind of fool, Elliot."

"Normally I'd ask precisely which kind of fool you do take me for," Burke said, fisting his hand around the receiver, "but I know how busy you always manage to be—and I don't think it's worth either your time or mine to trouble you for an answer."

"God," said Ken with a nasty chuckle. "If anything can drive Nora out of Montana and back home, it's you and that mind-numbing, so-called sense of humor. Put her on the line, Elliot."

"I'm afraid I can't do that at the moment. She's busy with the baby."

"Well, she won't be busy for long. Tell her to call me back. I'll be waiting."

"Does she have your number?"

Ken disconnected with a vicious oath, and Burke dropped the phone in its cradle.

Ashley's father hadn't once asked after her, damn him.

With a curse of his own, Burke swung away from the table to pace the room. According to Fitz, Ken had never visited Nora at the ranch. Had Ken tried to get Nora to come back to California so he could see his daughter? Had he ever sent any child support? Had he ever—

This was none of Burke's business. None of it.

But, oh, God, he wanted it to be his business—even if he knew he'd never be able to line up these figures in tidy rows. For now, he could only hope he hadn't added fuel to Ken's ire, that the volatile man wouldn't vent his frustration and anger in Nora's direction.

He walked to Nora's doorway a few minutes later, struggling to keep his expression blank. "Ken would like you to call him as soon as you get a chance."

She tensed, and Ashley whooped. Nora shifted the baby and reached for his hand, but he slipped his hands into his pockets and moved to stare out the window.

"I'll call him back after I'm finished here," she said.

Burke nodded and left the room, shutting the door behind him.

AN HOUR LATER Burke pulled his jacket from the closet as Nora carried Ashley into his room. He wanted to stay with Nora, to make sure she was going to be all right now that she'd finished talking with Ken, but he had to leave to pick up Fitz's family at the airport. "He wants to see his daughter, doesn't he?"

"Did he tell you that?"

Burke shook his head. "No. But what else could it be?"

Nora paced with the baby, patting her back. "I don't know what to do."

"Don't you?"

"Why should I?"

"You must know what to expect. You were married to him for nearly two years."

Burke regretted his words the moment he uttered them. He wasn't himself, not with this vague panic pressing in on him like a vise. He didn't care for the sensation, especially now that he realized he couldn't seem to control his reactions any more than he could control the situation.

She shot him a narrow-eyed glance. "Just because two people are married doesn't mean they understand everything about each other."

"What will you do?"

She rested her cheek on Ashley's hand. "I'll let him see her. He is her father."

"Yes, he is." Burke shoved his arms into the jacket sleeves with slow, precise movements. If he made the wrong move right now, he'd shatter into a million jagged pieces. "He has a right to see her. To spend time with her, to get to know her."

"He says he wants an extended visit." Her face paled, and she sank to the bed. "Oh, God, Burke. He doesn't know her. He doesn't know how to take care of her, how she likes to be rocked to sleep, how to—he can't feed her."

He slid his hands into his pockets and they stared at each other in taut silence, sharing the misery.

"Is he asking for time alone with her?"

Her throat worked as she tried to speak, and a tear spilled from one of those large, exotic, tragic eyes. "What if he does?"

"You could provide a bottle," he said, wishing again that he didn't have to go.

"Not that many."

He couldn't imagine what Nora must be going through. The thought of handing Ashley over to Ken paralyzed him with fear. And rage and helplessness—and a terrible, overwhelming envy that burned and gnawed through his gut.

Nora rocked and held her daughter so tightly she squirmed and whimpered. "Shh, baby. It's going to be all right."

Burke lowered his head and stared at the floor. He wished he could believe it.

CHAPTER NINETEEN

NORA WAS RELIEVED when Burke left for the ranch house after a late breakfast on Tuesday morning. She was expecting Ken, and she didn't want to have to deal with one more source of stress layered over the coming confrontation.

The open-ended agreement about visitations had been a mistake. Setting limits was the only way to deal with the problem.

And moving back to California was the only way to make those limits stick.

There Ken was now, driving up the rise in his rental car. She pulled on a jacket and stepped out on the porch to meet him.

"Hello, Nora."

"Hello, Ken." She crossed her arms and waited for him to climb the steps. "Ashley's asleep. She has a difficult day ahead of her, and I don't want her disturbed."

"Okay. Fine." He paused. "Aren't you going to ask me in?"

"We can talk out here."

"It's freezing out here."

She narrowed her eyes. "What do you want?"

"I told you on the phone. I want to see her."

"You said you wanted to take her for an extended visit."

He huffed out an impatient breath. "It doesn't have to be that extended."

"How extended does it have to be?"

"Come on, Nora. Be reasonable. That's all I'm asking for," he said with one of his oh-so-charming smiles. "A reasonable amount of time with my own daughter. Alone, if possible."

She tugged her jacket more tightly around her middle, shivering from the chill of his voice. "You don't know how to take care of her."

"I could figure it out if you'd let me spend time with her."

"I didn't say you couldn't. I'm saying you don't know how to take care of a baby."

He tugged the collar of his jacket up around his ears. "I can find out."

"She's not something to practice on."

Another chill slicked through her when Burke's SUV nosed over the rise and coasted to a stop beside Ken's car.

Ken shot a dark glance at the car and turned back to her. "How much did you know about taking care of a baby before you did it the first time?"

"I had help."

"I can get help, too."

"So, you're not going to take care of her yourself."

"I thought you weren't happy with that idea. Now you're not happy with the alternative." He waved a hand and moved away from her before wheeling back. "A perfectly reasonable alternative, one you've as good as admitted to resorting to yourself."

"You don't understand. It's not the same thing."

Ken took a menacing step closer. "Why don't you explain it, then?"

AS HE STEPPED from his car, Burke heard the weary frustration in Nora's voice and the rising anger in Ken's. When he saw Ken leaning toward her, something inside him snapped.

Before he realized what he was doing, he

scooped up a handful of snow and squeezed it into a compact ball.

"You're not making any sense," said Ken. "I think we—"

The fat white lump of snow slammed into the side of his face.

"What the…" Ken slapped at the wet mush sliding down his neck and into his jacket collar. "Where did that come from?"

Nora bit her lower lip and stared as Burke shaped another snowball, his eyes narrowed at Ken.

"This conversation is over," said Burke.

"Did you throw that at me?" Ken's face reddened to match the splotchy area near his ear where the snowball had hit. "What the hell are you doing, Elliot?"

"Getting your attention."

"You got it. Now you can get the hell out of here and let me finish talking to my wife."

"Your ex-wife."

"Just because you're sleeping with her doesn't—"

The second snowball hit Ken square in the chest. He pointed a finger at Burke. "That's assault."

"That's snow." Burke shook clumps of slush from his gloves as he waded through the drift toward the porch. "I'd be happy to show you the difference."

Nora stepped between the men and shoved a palm against Burke's chest. "Don't. He's not worth the trouble he'd cause."

"I'm not the one causing the trouble here." Ken brushed melting flakes from his jacket. "I'm not the one throwing snowballs like some playground bully."

Burke didn't take his eyes off Ken. "If you have something to say to Nora, you'll say it in a respectful tone of voice."

Nora gave him a tiny shove. "I can take care of myself."

Ken took her arm but dropped it when Burke shifted past her. "You're the one who's not welcome here, Elliot. This is a private conversation. About our daughter."

"Burke," said Nora. *"Please."*

He stared at her, as stiff and cold, as miserable and frightened as he'd been when he'd walked through the blizzard in the dark. "I'll be out by the woodpile if you need me."

"She doesn't need you, Elliot." Ken opened the door behind her. "She doesn't need anyone. She got the baby she wanted, and that's all she cares about."

Burke continued to stare at her for a long,

empty moment, and then he backed off the porch and trudged around the corner of the cabin.

NORA CRUNCHED through the deep snow half an hour later, following Burke's path to ease her way.

Motherhood had changed her. With her daughter's future at stake, she'd taken control of the situation with Ken, making several demands of her own—and he'd quickly agreed to them all after the first wriggling, wailing diaper change.

Now she had to take control, somehow, of the situation with Burke. "Easier said than done," she muttered as she stretched from one deep, Burke-sized footprint to another. But in the midst of all the complicated, unresolved matters between them, there was one very simple thing to do: sign the contract.

Was it just a few days ago she'd thought that document represented all the biggest problems in her life?

She found Burke beneath the sloping shed roof, restacking the firewood into slightly neater piles. "Why did you come back?" she asked. "You knew Ken would be here."

He straightened and stared at her, his

breath billowing out in a white cloud. "You told me Ashley had a doctor's appointment today. I came to take you both into town, as I'd promised. To offer a little moral support."

Oh, dear. Dear, dear Burke. Why did he make everything so hard by making every little thing so easy?

She sank to perch on one of the stumps and the cold began to seep into her. He glanced toward the bedroom window. "Is he in there? With her?"

"Yes."

Burke turned back to his unnecessary chore.

Nora twisted her hands together. "I've asked him to go with me to the doctor's office."

"I understand." He looked at her over his shoulder with the merest trace of a smile, and it squeezed at her heart to see what that small gesture was costing him.

"Go ahead," he said. "It'll be dark by the time you get back. I'll leave the lights on for you."

BURKE HAD ASKED HIMSELF some hard questions during the strained take-out burger dinner for three at the cabin, a dinner eaten in shifts while each of them took turns trying to comfort the howling baby. Would this be the pattern of his life? Forming part of an uneasy threesome? Forced to stand impotently on the sidelines while Ken and Nora battled over parenting issues?

Shortly after the dinner mess was cleared away, Ken had announced he'd had enough and was heading back to Butte, and Nora had collapsed in tears when he walked out the door. Burke had gathered her close, even as he wondered if he wanted to spend the rest of his life picking up the pieces after one of Ken's visits.

And did he want to continue to be a target for the tabloids? He'd made light of his television appearance, but it had shaken him more than he'd admitted.

He was still asking questions late that night, while he reached deep for patience as Ashley strained and arched against him. The side of his face was moist with her tears, and his gut twisted with the shaky, echoing pitch of her screams. "Shh, shh," he whispered, though he knew she couldn't hear him over the wails of her own distress and wouldn't understand him if she could. "It's going to be all right."

"But what if it isn't?" Nora, pale and wild-eyed with worry, paced across the room.

"What if the vaccine is making her sick? What if she's having some sort of an allergic reaction? She might be—"

"The doctor warned you she might run a bit of a fever and be a little uncomfortable." Burke stroked his hand over the back of the baby's head, trying to coax her to snuggle into his shoulder. "This is exactly what he told you to expect."

"But how can I be sure?" Nora moved in close to pat Ashley's back. "She feels so warm. Maybe her temperature is going up. If it gets too high she could have a seizure."

"Do you want to take it again?" He thought he sounded reasonable and reassuring, though he was beginning to panic.

"No." Nora dragged her hands through her hair. "I just don't know what to do."

He set the baby on the bed and began to tug her nightie over her head.

"What are you doing?" asked Nora.

"She's working herself into a sweat with all the crying, and holding her against me makes her warmer." He winced as she coughed and choked through a particularly nasty scream. "I'm going to try to cool her off."

"Don't let her get chilled."

"I wouldn't do that, would I?" he asked the baby.

He brushed one of her little disposable wipes lightly over her belly, and then he climbed into bed with her and pulled the covers over them both.

Nora slid in on the opposite side, and they stretched out with the baby between them, as they had for all the nights of the storm. They comforted Ashley while she kicked and hiccupped and wailed, and he told Nora tales from his boarding-school days to distract her.

Eventually the baby quieted enough to nurse, and she fell asleep during the meal. Nora's eyelids drifted closed shortly after.

Burke lay in the dark, staring at them both and asking himself more questions. They needed him, didn't they? And didn't he need them? How could he live his life without them? Without his special friend and the baby he'd come to love? How could he miss out on seeing Ashley grow into a woman as lovely as her mother?

He curled himself around their sleeping forms as best he could and lay there, listening to them breathe, relaxing for the first time since Ken had called. Loving them both so very much, loving them with every breath of his own.

And there in that last thought of the day, in that last breath before sleep, he found the answers to all his questions.

BURKE WOKE BEFORE DAWN to find Nora's side of the bed empty and Ashley snoring lightly in her crib.

He tiptoed down the hall to the front room. Nora was seated at the kitchen table, sipping a mug of coffee. The script lay open near her elbow.

"Good morning," he said as he bent to kiss her forehead.

She didn't move; she didn't react.

"I'm sorry about…about Ken," she said. "I'm sorry about the way things turned out, with the doctor's visit and…everything. I didn't stop to think about how you might react. I didn't understand that you might be angry. Or jealous."

"I was. Both."

"I figured that out." She took another sip. "The snowball was my first hint."

His smile felt more like a grimace. "Not my best moment."

"No. But an important one, for me."

She set down the mug and stared into the coffee. "I've been sitting here, thinking about what I'll have to deal with in the coming months. It's a lot to handle all at once. A lot of priorities, a lot of prioritizing. I wish I had your talent with lists," she said with a glance in his direction.

There had been nothing warm or friendly in that glance, and Burke grew cold. He thought he knew where this discussion was headed, and he searched for a way to knock it off track.

"There's one person who has to come before all the others," said Nora. "One person I need to put at the top of all my lists, one person whose needs have to come before mine. And I need to be there for her, one hundred percent."

She remained uncommonly still—no tilting head, no flashing hands or expressively arching brows. She made no movements at all but for her fingers tightening on the mug. "You've made a career—several careers—out of being the responsible one. The grown-up in any group."

He cleared his throat. "You make it sound like a liability."

"It's not. It's a fine and admirable thing. And you do it so well."

"The fine and admirable part?"

"All of it."

The look she gave him made him wonder if she'd truly meant what she'd said.

"But it's my turn now," she continued. "Maybe not the fine and admirable part, but the rest of it, that grown-up part. I'm trying to do things for myself now, to be the responsible person in my daughter's life."

He struggled to force his words through a throat gone tight and dry. "And there can be only one of those people in her life at a time, is that it?"

"No, of course not. But I think perhaps I should try it that way for a while."

She spread her hand over the script and paused, as if waiting for some reaction from him. Her eyes, when she lifted them to meet his, gave him no hint what that reaction should be.

"I see," he said, though he didn't. Not at all.

And in the next moment, he saw it was too late.

Strange, this tunnel-like view of his dreams fading before his eyes. As if he stood at one side of a mountain and she at the other, with their words echoing in the long, hollow space between them.

"If you'll excuse me," he said, "I'll go take a shower."

She raised her mug to her lips again, and he walked away.

HE MIGHT GO QUIETLY, he decided when the hot water pummeled some feeling back into his numbed body and some sense into his panicked brain, but he wouldn't stay that way for long. He wouldn't be calm, and logical and patient. He wouldn't be polite, and cooperative and docile, not anymore. Not for Nora, not for any of them.

His mind raced through plans and details, his thoughts concentrated on checking lists and prioritizing items as he dressed in a white shirt and black slacks and packed his suitcases. And then he pulled on his blue parka and carried his things to the front room, where he found Nora waiting for him, holding a legal-sized document.

"I'm leaving," he said, though he figured the suitcases, like the snowball, had already given her a hint. He stared at the white papers in her hand. "I think I can catch that afternoon flight Ken spoke of."

"I've signed the contract," she said. "You can take it with you."

"All right." He set his briefcase on the table, near one of Ashley's brightly colored toys, and placed the paperwork she gave him inside. "If you think that will make things easier."

"I never meant to make them so hard," she said, and her voice wavered enough to give him a sliver of hope.

He gave her the best smile he could manage. "You don't have to feel guilty."

"*Burke.*" She blew out his name on a short, weary laugh. "You always know exactly what to say."

She hesitated, just for a moment, and then she pressed a brief, sweet, friendly kiss against his cheek. "Have a safe trip. See you soon."

She disappeared around the corner, and a moment later he heard the soft click of her bedroom door closing.

CHAPTER TWENTY

BURKE DRAGGED his luggage behind him through the main entrance of Bert Mooney Airport near Butte. It seemed as though it had been some other man, an imposter living inside his skin, who'd passed through these same doors twelve days ago. A successful, confident, colorless man, a man whose narrow view of life could encompass only his job and his tidy plan for getting it accomplished.

The man who collected his ticket to Los Angeles, checked his things and walked into the small snack area today was a man whose baby-spit-upon life was in catastrophic emotional upheaval, kaleidoscopic in its ruin, rich with irony and the potential for extremes of suffering and joy. And his considerably altered view included the one human being standing between him and the messy, sprawling plan he hoped to accomplish.

"Hello, Ken."

Ken glanced up and then hunched again over his cocktail. "What are you doing here?"

"Looking for you." Burke gestured to the space next to Ken. "Mind if I join you?"

Ken grunted a neutral response, and Burke slid onto the stool and signaled for the bartender. "Bushmills, neat. And another round here."

"Thanks," said Ken, and then he tossed back the rest of his drink.

Burke folded his arms on the bar. "Sorry about the snowball. I haven't been myself lately."

Ken shrugged it off. "She has that effect on people."

"Yes, she does." Burke took a tiny, companionable sip of the whiskey he didn't want and set the glass aside. "But that's not why I did it. When I saw you standing there, I knew that no matter what happened between Nora and me, you'd always be there. Standing on the porch."

"We're divorced."

"You're Ashley's father."

"Not if Nora has anything to say about it."

"She'll come round. She'll realize that Ashley needs you in her life."

Ken twisted his glass on the counter. "I didn't want the baby."

"I know."

"I would have wanted one eventually, just not... right now."

"But you've got one now," Burke pointed out. "And you came a long way to make a start with her."

Ken aimed an accusing look in his direction and picked up his glass. "That's not why I came."

Burke nodded, offering an unspoken truce. "But is that why you're leaving?"

The bartender refilled the bowl of pretzels in front of them and moved down the counter.

Burke leaned in closer. "Would waiting— waiting to have a baby—would it have made a difference, do you think?"

"I'll never know." Ken frowned at his drink and then nearly finished it in one swallow. "We had some good times. Had some bad ones, even before the baby."

"Most marriages are like that, I think."

"Most marriages aren't made in Hollywood."

Burke decided he wanted a bit of his whiskey after all.

"That Ashley," said Ken after a while. "She sure is a looker."

"Just like her mom."

"Yeah." Ken drained his glass. "Exactly like her mom."

"No, not exactly." Burke stared at the amber fluid in his glass. "She's got your nose."

"You think?"

"That's not all she got from you." Burke shifted to face him. "She's going to want to know you, Ken. To spend time with you. Because no matter what her mother does, no matter how many men, how many people come into and go out of her life, you're the only person on the face of the earth who is her *father*."

Ken rubbed his hand across his mouth. "I thought it would be easier to stay away, at first. Nora wanted me to, and…" He blew out a breath. "I let too much time go by making too many excuses. The fact is, this is all so damn hard. So much harder than I thought it would be. Nora and…and the baby."

He stared at Burke. "I don't know how to be her father. Especially from a distance."

"I don't think it will be as hard as you think." Burke shoved his glass aside. "Call her once a week, just for a couple of minutes, just to say hello. Jot it down in your appointment calendar so you won't forget. Send her a gift at Christmas and on her birthday. Ask Nora to remind you—and she will, since she won't want her daughter to be disappointed."

"A gift?"

"Have your secretary pick something out, if you can't manage it yourself. Jewelry is a safe choice. Jody seems to enjoy the simple pieces Fitz gives her."

He waited, and Ken nodded.

"Give her your phone number. And then be there for her when she calls." Burke fingered his napkin. "You could tell her she's a looker, every once in a while."

"Yeah, she'd probably like to hear that."

"Any woman would like to hear that from any man." Burke forced himself to look at the man sitting next to him, to accept the emotion making his next words so hard to get past the hot, swelling part of his throat. "I imagine a young girl needs to hear it from her father first."

"What about you?" Ken shoved his empty glass aside. "Where do you fit into this cozy picture?"

"I'm not sure." Burke set the rest of his drink on the counter untouched, his gut burning from more than the alcohol. "Even if I were lucky enough to earn a spot in the family group, I'll never be Ashley's father."

"You'd like that, wouldn't you?"

"I'd give anything to call that little girl my own."

Burke stood and pulled his wallet from his back pocket. "Now you know the reason for the snowball. It had nothing to do with Nora, and everything to do with what I realized the moment I saw you standing there. The reality of what you'll always be to Ashley. Something I can never replace."

He tossed a few bills on the bar. "You may not be feeling this way today, but you're a very lucky man, Ken. I envy you that."

He turned to go.

"Elliot."

"Yeah?"

"Good luck. With Nora."

"Thanks." He slipped his hands into his pockets. "I'll need it."

BURKE WATCHED a pair of headlights swing into the parking area near the front door of his studio bungalow late that night. He stood behind his desk and waited for his boss to enter.

"This better be good." Fitz tossed his

duffel on the sofa and headed into the tiny kitchen for the coffee steaming on the counter. "I've been on the set since five this morning, and I'd like to get home and climb into bed before my alarm goes off for tomorrow's call."

"You won't be getting any sympathy from me about sleepless nights."

"Oh. That's right," said Fitz as he sprawled on the sofa and stacked his feet on the arm. "You spent two weeks cooped up with a baby, and now you're the expert on sleep deprivation." He sampled his coffee. "Welcome back, by the way."

"Thanks."

"I take it your sudden appearance means the mission was successful?"

"I'll fill you in when Greenberg gets here."

Fitz sighed. "Don't tell me you're going to try to quit again."

"No."

"Good." Fitz drained his cup and rolled to his side. "Then wake me when the meeting's over."

Greenberg burst through the door, a cigar clamped between his teeth and the knot in his necktie tugged to one side. "Make it fast, Elliot. I've got an appointment."

"At ten o'clock at night?" Fitz shoved

upright with a groan. "You're working too hard, Myron. You'll have a heart attack, and then where will you be?"

"In the ground." Burke moved from behind his desk to hand two folders to each of his visitors. "I won't keep you long. In the first folder, you'll find a copy of Nora's contract with Big Sky Entertainment. You'll see I've noted a few additions and corrections, but it's nothing we can't live with."

"You did it." Greenberg gritted his teeth in his version of a smile. "It's about time."

"And in the second folder, you'll find a draft of a contract describing my promotion to full partnership in the corporation."

"What?" Greenberg nearly dropped his cigar. "What the—"

"Wait a minute." Fitz flipped through his copy. "Why are you doing this?"

"Because if I'm going to continue being caught in the middle between the two of you, I'm going to do it from the middle. Not from the outside, and not from the position of an at-will employee."

"Now, you listen here, Ell—"

"Myron," said Burke as he raised his hand, "you've taken on more than you can handle here. As long as you choose to keep your agency as a going concern, that has to be your first priority. You need someone in this office who can help you keep Fitz in line. Someone who has the authority to do it."

"Damn right I do. This son of a—"

"Fitz," said Burke, "you're constantly racing between film sets in California and elsewhere and a ranch in Montana, and you're about to become a father. I think you're going to want to spend more time with your child than you've been able to carve out for your wife."

"Don't you start lecturing—"

"I've come to the conclusion," said Burke, "that Casey is perfectly capable of assisting with the preproduction budget process, as Myron assured me when he hired her."

"What did you think I—"

"And I'm prepared to let her continue in that position," said Burke, "with a few minor alterations to her job description and office location. However, she doesn't have the benefit of my contacts here at Paramount. My very useful and important contacts. My very *appreciative* contacts."

"The contacts who'll hire you away from us," said Fitz, "if we give you any trouble over this."

"That's right."

The actor frowned at the contract in his hands as Greenberg paced and swore. "Is this what you want?"

"Yes."

"I see it includes a hefty raise."

"I'll be needing it," said Burke. "And you can afford it, considering how much I'm going to earn for you on the next project."

"Got one in mind?"

"More than one. That's why I'm going to take an immediate leave of absence. In Montana."

Fitz grinned. "For how long?"

Burke handed him a pen. "For as long as it takes."

NORA PACED a step-swing, step-swing circle around the softly lit second parlor of the ranch house on Thursday night, patting Ashley's back and waiting for a second burp as the baby settled, warm and heavy, against her shoulder. In the dining room, Maggie and Jody argued over a school disciplinary policy while they set the table for dinner with the everyday china.

No need for anything special tonight. No visitors from California. No place set for Burke to even out the odd-numbered spot set for her.

No, no place for Burke. Not in her bed, not anymore. No more sweet moments of shared memories and laughter and loving. She'd done a terrific job of sending him packing, contract and all—and he'd packed and raced out her door without a backward glance. How very neat and tidy of him.

And if she missed him and wanted him back with an irrational intensity beyond anything she'd imagined possible, well, it was only what she deserved for treating him so poorly while he was here.

Poor, poor Burke.

Ashley managed a quiet burp without too much fuss. She stilled and sagged, and Nora wandered into the entry to peek in the hat-rack mirror. Her daughter's eyes drooped in slo-mo.

"Looks like she might sleep through dinner," Ellie whispered when she stepped out of the office. "You can relax and enjoy your meal."

"I'm not that hungry." Nora sighed and glanced at Ashley in the mirror again. Almost asleep. "I shouldn't have come."

"That would have been a mistake. It's a lot less complicated to skimp on servings than to skip one of Mom's family dinners."

Nora buried her face in Ashley's neck. "I'm going to miss this. All of it."

"We're going to miss you, too." Ellie stroked the baby's hair. "But I have a feeling that between Mom and Fitz, we're all going to get hauled out to L.A. on a regular basis to check up on you."

"I'd like that."

"I'll remind you what you just said, someday."

Nora followed her through the parlors and slipped Ashley into her car seat in a corner beside the ornately carved buffet. They'd be ready to make a quick escape once the meal was finished. Or nearly finished, since Nora would be skipping dessert tonight to save on calories and get an early start on her packing.

The talk around the table seemed to lack its usual energy. No news from school, no scandals in town, a lull in the calving and a break in the weather. Ashley continued her unexpected early nap in her seat, until the dogs scrambled across the porch to leap down the steps, barking at some unseen intruder. Her eyes opened wide, and she gulped in air and let out a howl.

"What are those fool dogs after now?" asked Will as he plucked the baby from her carrier.

Wayne tipped back in his chair to peer out the window. "Someone's coming up the road."

BURKE STEPPED from his rental car near the front porch of the Granite Ridge ranch house and glared at Rowdy. He pointed a finger at the yapping pup. *"Down."*

The little dog tucked his tail between his legs and slunk away.

Jenna slipped through the big entry door, rubbing her hands over her arms. "Burke? Is that you?"

"Yes, Jenna. It's me. Again."

"We didn't expect you," she said as he climbed the steps. "But there's plenty for dinner, if you'd like to join us."

"Thank you." He took her arm and pressed a kiss to her cheek, and she pulled back with a surprised smile. "I appreciate that."

"It *is* Burke. I knew it." Jody bounded from her spying post near the entry staircase and dashed toward the dining room. "Hey, everyone. Burke is here."

He hung his jacket on a hall tree hook and followed Jenna through the parlors, headed toward the group gathered beneath the amber glow of the old gaslight chandelier. They were all here but Fitz, of course. Maggie and Wayne, holding hands under the tablecloth between courses. Jenna and Will, sending each other silent signals across the length of the family table. Ellie, tugging Jody back into her seat with a hissing comment about manners. Ashley, peering at him from Will's arms, her eyes showing traces of unhappy tears. And Nora, sitting in her assigned seat and looking very nearly serene as he approached.

Why had he ever thought he desired serenity in a woman, when flash and fire could add so much warmth to life?

"Evening, Burke," said Will as he shifted Ashley to pass a basket heaped with Jenna's homemade rolls to Jody. "Good to see you."

"Hello, Will. Hello, everyone." He raked his fingers through his hair, scattering a few tiny droplets of melted snow. "Sorry for the intrusion. I won't be long, I promise."

"Please, have a seat." Jenna handed a platter of thick, pink roast beef slices to Wayne and gestured at the empty spot beside Jody. "Have you eaten?"

"I didn't come for dinner," he said. "And I'd prefer to stand, if that's all right. I have something to say to Nora. Something to ask her."

The normal bustle around the table

quieted to a near hush. Even Ashley muffled herself by attempting to wedge her fat little fist into her mouth.

Nora straightened and picked up her water glass—a handy prop to embellish her regal gesture for him to proceed.

"I found Ken at the airport yesterday," said Burke. "He and I have reached an understanding, of sorts."

"How nice for you both." She paused for a sip, staring at him over the rim.

"I'd like to reach an understanding with you, too, if possible."

She studied the glass with a tiny frown. "I thought you said this wasn't going to take long."

"Ouch," said Jody.

"Jody." Jenna sighed and sent Burke a pleading look. "Are you sure you won't have some dessert, at least? How about some coffee?"

"How about some privacy?" asked Will.

"No, let's hear what he has to say." Maggie tossed her napkin on the table and leaned back in her chair.

"You might want to get down on one knee," said Wayne. He stretched his arm along the back of his wife's chair. "Worked for me."

"Yes, a little desperation would be a nice touch." Maggie gave him one of her sassy grins. "And, Nora, you go ahead and keep playing hard to get."

"Please." Ellie rolled her eyes. "Don't encourage them. These Hollywood types are always turning everything into a production as it is."

"Have you got a ring?" asked Jody.

"No." Burke shoved his glasses a bit higher on his nose and leveled his gaze at Nora. "We could go shopping for one together. I thought we'd just wander up and down the jewelry store aisles, figure out what we need and toss it into the cart."

"Oh." Nora's hand trembled as she lowered her glass to the table. "I like the sound of that."

"Go, Burke," said Ellie with a grin.

He nodded and took a deep breath. "Over the past two weeks I've asked you to come back to California for your house and your friends, for a part in a movie and for the sake of your career. In the best interests of your daughter. I came here tonight to ask you to come back for *me*."

She sank her teeth into her lush lower lip. "It may be an absolute disaster."

"I'm counting on it."

He cleared his throat as he stepped farther into the room. "The question I want to ask you—the thing I want to know—is if you think you can accept things the way they are."

"The way they are?"

She struggled to hide her dismay, but she wasn't a good enough actress to cover it completely. He knew she'd expected a marriage proposal.

They all had.

He didn't intend to disappoint any of them. But first he needed to reach that understanding.

To be very, very precise.

"The way they are," he repeated. "We've been friends a long time, Nora. No matter what happens between us, I don't want to lose that friendship."

He took another step toward her. "I don't want to lose my *best friend.*"

"Oh," she said again, and her eyes were suspiciously bright. "I like the sound of that, too."

"I'm glad to hear it," he said with a smile. "So now the next question is—do you think it's possible to love a friend the way I love you and still call her a friend?"

"I hope so," she whispered, "because I love you, too."

Jenna sniffed into her napkin. Ellie and Jody smiled at each other with matching grins, and Maggie dragged Wayne's hand from beneath the table and squeezed it over her heart.

Burke slipped his hands into his pockets. "Have we reached an understanding, then?"

One of the tears swimming in Nora's eyes darted down the graceful curve of her cheek. She parted her lips as if to answer, but swallowed again and nodded instead.

"I'm glad for that, too." He smiled. "Because your friendship will always mean as much to me as your love."

He glanced at Wayne. "On one knee, did you say?"

Wayne shrugged. "Seems to me you're doing okay without it."

"Did Fitz get down on one knee for you, Mom?" asked Jody.

"Nope." Ellie frowned. "He didn't have a ring, either."

"Loser," said Jody. "What about you, Gran? How did Will propose?"

Above her napkin, Jenna's face turned a bright pink.

"That's between your Gran and me. Here," he said as he handed a fussing Ashley to Maggie. "Your turn."

Burke smiled at the noisy, nosy group seated around the table, enjoying the way the conversation disintegrated to drift over various family memories. He'd miss them all, he knew. Nora certainly would. He'd have to make it up to her, to make an effort to fill the seats around their own dining-room table with friends and family.

He pulled Ashley from Maggie's arms. Lots and lots of family.

Nora crooked her finger at him, and he rock-rock-rocked his way to her side, patting Ashley's back.

"Don't you have any other questions for me?" she asked.

"Just one. Do you want me to get down on one knee while I ask it?"

"I don't think that's necessary." She lifted her napkin to brush at a line of white-flecked drool sliding down his shirt front. "The fact that you can take this without flinching makes a nice impression of its own."

"In that case, I'll skip straight to the proposal." He shifted the baby higher on his shoulder and reached for her hand. "Marry me, Nora. Let's wreak havoc on what's left of our lives."

She tugged at his hand and pulled him down for a kiss, and the baby squirmed between them. "Yes, Burke, I'll marry you."

"I like the sound of that." He kissed her again. "Come home with me. Tomorrow."

Her smile was dazzling. "All right."

"Sit down, Burke," said Jenna. She smiled as she arranged a place setting of her everyday china for him, with pieces she'd collected from the kitchen.

He took his seat at the crowded table and settled the baby in his lap, enjoying the feel of her snug little body warming his.

Family had never felt so fine.

* * * * *

*Mills & Boon® Supperromance
brings you a special preview…*

In How To Trap a Parent *movie publicist Jane
Linden returns to Red Hill, eager to sell her late
aunt's farm and cut all ties with the town she
fled, pregnant and alone, twelve years earlier. If
only the local real-estate agent wasn't her former
teen sweetheart…and their respective kids
weren't plotting to make them fall in love again!*

*Turn the page for a sneak peek at this
fantastic new story from Joan Kilby,
available next month in
Mills & Boon® Supperromance.*

How To Trap a Parent
by
Joan Kilby

JANE LINDEN PARKED her black Mazda in front of Red Hill Real Estate and checked her hair in the visor mirror. Just her luck! The only person in this small rural town who could sell her late aunt's farm for her was Cole Roberts, the man who'd broken her heart thirteen years ago. Cole wasn't a *bad* man; in fact, she'd never known anyone as loyal to his family. But that didn't mean he hadn't made her suffer.

Hitching her red leather tote higher on her shoulder, Jane climbed out of the car. Seeing him again would *not* be a problem. She was *over* him; him and his green eyes and killer grin. She'd be in and out of Red Hill faster than she could snap her fingers. And he would never know she'd cried herself to sleep for three years because he'd married Leslie Stanwyck instead of her.

All that had happened a long time ago. Jane was a different person, older and wiser. She might not have made a name for herself in Hollywood, but those acting lessons Rafe had given her way back when were finally going to pay off. Bright and breezy, that's the way she'd play it. Ignore the pain, hide the anger; Cole no longer meant a thing to her. How could he? Thirteen years was way too long to carry a torch.

A bell tinkled as she entered through the glass door of the real estate agency. A small seating area was to her right, reception to her left. The young woman behind the curved desk wore black rectangular glasses and had fine dark hair swept into a ponytail.

Leslie's little sister. The last time Jane had seen this girl she'd worn pigtails and Bratz T-shirts. Jane pushed her sunglasses up into her hair. "Millie?"

Millie glanced up with a bright smile. "Hi, um… Do I know you?"

"Jane Linden. I went to high school

with Leslie." She glanced past reception to the narrow hall and the private offices. "Is Cole in?"

"I'll see if he's available." Millie reached for the phone.

"He and I are old friends. I'll surprise him." Jane hurried past before Millie could stop her. Old friends, indeed. They'd been far more to each other than friends; and in the end, far less.

Through the glass wall of his office she could see Cole working on something at his desk, his brow creased in concentration as he chewed on the end of a pencil. In spite of her pep talk, her heart turned over at the sight of his face, still familiar even though she hadn't seen him in three years, the time he'd come to L.A. to visit Mary Kate.

Steeling herself, she knocked once and opened the door. "Well, just look at you! All dressed up in a suit and tie behind a big fancy desk. You're quite the successful businessman."

Cole started at her voice, his eyebrows lifting as he set aside his pencil and newspaper. He smoothed a hand lightly over his neatly combed dark brown hair. "Jane! I'm surprised to see you back in Red Hill so soon." He glanced past her eagerly. "Did you bring Mary Kate this time?"

Jane had come alone four weeks earlier to arrange her aunt Esther's funeral. Mary Kate had stayed in L.A. with friends. She'd had the lead in the classroom concert as well as end-of-term exams.

"She's at the farmhouse." Jane's grip on her tote strap tightened. As the girl's father, Cole had rights whether she liked it or not. *Bright and breezy,* she reminded herself and pasted on a smile. "We arrived yesterday. We're both still jet-lagged so I let Mary Kate stay home."

"Have a seat," Cole said. "I'm sorry about your aunt Esther. She was so young."

"Thanks." Jane sat stiffly on the edge of the visitor's chair. "Her heart attack was unexpected."

"I'm sorry I missed the funeral," Cole continued formally. "I was closing a deal on a house that afternoon or I would've come. I called you the next day but you must have already left."

"I was only in town a few days," Jane explained, shifting in her chair. It was hard to be bright when the subject was so sad, hard to be breezy when the conversation was this stilted. "I had work commitments and wanted to be back for Christmas."

"How long are you in Australia?"

Jane forced herself to relax and sink back into the chair. Her short white skirt slid halfway up her thigh. She saw his gaze drop before he quickly glanced away. She tugged the fabric down. "We're back for good. Goodbye, L.A., hello, Melbourne. I've got a job as a publicist with Moonray Productions. In fact, I've hit the ground running, publicizing the premiere of a movie called *Swept Away.*"

"You mean it?" he said. "You're back?"

She nodded. "A moving company is packing up my house in Pasadena and shipping everything down here."

"That's wonderful news," Cole said, smiling for the first time. "I'll be able to get to know Mary Kate properly. Stephanie will be excited."

"How is Stephanie?" Jane asked politely. "Does she live with you?"

"She's great. She stays with me on the weekends and during the summer holidays and with Leslie during the week when school's in." He angled a framed photo on his desk so Jane could see the picture of a young girl with Cole's open grin and Leslie's straight blond hair. "She's turning twelve next month. Loves horses."

"Mary Kate, too," Jane said, softening.

"Yeah?" Cole's face lit.

Something like warmth flashed between them, a shared moment over their daughter. Then Cole leaned back in his chair, his face carefully neutral.

"Leslie's married to Fergus Palmer now," Cole went on. "They have two little boys from his first marriage."

"So I heard." Cole's divorce from Leslie had gone through before his trip to L.A. At first Jane had wondered if he'd been hoping to get back together with her, but his interest had proved to be solely in Mary Kate.

Cole glanced at her bare left hand. "What about you? Are you still seeing that producer you introduced me to in L.A.?"

"That was a long time ago. Anyway, I don't have time for a relationship," Jane said. "Mary Kate and I are a self-contained unit. We don't need anyone else."

Cole came upright with a thump of his chair legs on the mat. "You can't decide that for Mary Kate. She has family here. Me, Stephanie, her grandmother and her uncle Joey—"

Jane held up a hand, shifting back to the edge of her seat. Any hint of warmth had vanished and the time for polite chitchat was definitely over. "She'll see you all, don't worry."

They glared at each other, unmoving.

Then Cole let out a breath and flexed his shoulders. Unexpectedly, he gave her the grin that used to twist her heart into knots.

MILLS & BOON
*Super*ROMANCE

On sale 15th May 2009

THE PERFECT DAUGHTER
by Anna DeStefano

A man who faces danger every day can't be right for Maggie. She needs to walk away from sexy cop Matt Lebretti, but will keeping her heart safe rob her of her chance for happiness?

THE MILLIONAIRE'S PRIVATE AFFAIR
by Karina Bliss

Wealthy Luke Carter needs beautiful mayor Liz Light – not only to help him build his camp for underprivileged children, but to win the happiness he deserves!

LOOKING FOR SOPHIE
by Roz Denny Fox

Hot-shot detective Julian must help beautiful Garnet Patton find a missing five-year-old, but becoming part of the case could put his own family at risk.

HOW TO TRAP A PARENT
by Joan Kilby

Jane Linden is back in town to deal with an unwanted inheritance – and ignore her high-school sweetheart. Except their respective kids are conniving to help them fall in love again.

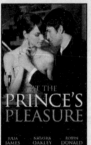

FREE

2 BOOKS AND A SURPRISE GIFT!

We would like to take this opportunity to thank you for reading this Mills & Boon® book by offering you the chance to take TWO more specially selected titles from the Superromance series absolutely FREE! We're also making this offer to introduce you to the benefits of the Mills & Boon® Book Club™ —

* ★ **FREE home delivery**
* ★ **FREE gifts and competitions**
* ★ **FREE monthly Newsletter**
* ★ **Books available before they're in the shops**
* ★ **Exclusive Mills & Boon Book Club offers**

Accepting these FREE books and gift places you under no obligation to buy; you may cancel at any time, even after receiving your free shipment. Simply complete your details below and return the entire page to the address below. You don't even need a stamp!

YES! Please send me 2 free Superromance books and a surprise gift. I understand that unless you hear from me, I will receive 4 superb new titles every month for just £3.69 each, postage and packing free. I am under no obligation to purchase any books and may cancel my subscription at any time. The free books and gift will be mine to keep in any case.

U9ZEE

Ms/Mrs/Miss/Mr...Initials ....
BLOCK CAPITALS PLEASE

Surname ....

Address ....

....

....Postcode ....

Send this whole page to:
The Mills & Boon Book Club, FREEPOST CN81, Croydon, CR9 3WZ